Maurice Procter and The Murder Room

>>> This title is part of The Murder Room, our series dedicated to making available out-of-print or hard-to-find titles by classic crime writers.

Crime fiction has always held up a mirror to society. The Victorians were fascinated by sensational murder and the emerging science of detection; now we are obsessed with the forensic detail of violent death. And no other genre has so captivated and enthralled readers.

Vast troves of classic crime writing have for a long time been unavailable to all but the most dedicated frequenters of second-hand bookshops. The advent of digital publishing means that we are now able to bring you the backlists of a huge range of titles by classic and contemporary crime writers, some of which have been out of print for decades.

From the genteel amateur private eyes of the Golden Age and the femmes fatales of pulp fiction, to the morally ambiguous hard-boiled detectives of mid twentieth-century America and their descendants who walk our twenty-first century streets, The Murder Room has it all. **>>>**

The Murder Room
Where Criminal Minds Meet

themurderroom.com

T0352278

Maurice Procter 1906–1973

Born in Nelson, Lancashire, Maurice Procter attended the local grammar school and ran away to join the army at the age of fifteen. In 1927 he joined the police in Yorkshire and served in the force for nineteen years before his writing was published and he was able to write full-time. He was credited with an ability to write exciting stories while using his experience to create authentic detail. His procedural novels are set in Granchester, a fictional 1950s Manchester, and he is best known for his series characters, Detective Superintendent Philip Hunter and DCI Harry Martineau. Throughout his career, Procter's novels increased in popularity in both the UK and the US, and in 1960 *Hell is a City* was made into a film starring Stanley Baker and Billie Whitelaw. Procter was married to Winifred, and they had one child, Noel.

Philip Hunter

The Chief Inspector's Statement (1951)
   aka *The Pennycross Murders*
I Will Speak Daggers (1956)
   aka *The Ripper*

Chief Inspector Martineau

Hell is a City (1954)
   aka *Somewhere in This City*
The Midnight Plumber (1957)
Man in Ambush (1958)
Killer at Large (1959)

Devil's Due (1960)
The Devil Was Handsome (1961)
A Body to Spare (1962)
Moonlight Flitting (1963)
  aka *The Graveyard Rolls*
Two Men in Twenty (1964)
Homicide Blonde (1965)
  aka *Death has a Shadow*
His Weight in Gold (1966)
Rogue Running (1966)
Exercise Hoodwink (1967)
Hideaway (1968)

Standalone Novels
Each Man's Destiny (1947)
No Proud Chivalry (1947)
The End of the Street (1949)
Hurry the Darkness (1952)
Rich is the Treasure (1952)
  aka *Diamond Wizard*
The Pub Crawler (1956)
Three at the Angel (1958)
The Spearhead Death (1960)
Devil in Moonlight (1962)
The Dog Man (1969)

Man in Ambush

Maurice Procter

An Orion book

Copyright © Maurice Procter 1958

The right of Maurice Procter to be identified as the author of this work
has been asserted in accordance with the Copyright, Designs and Patents
Act 1988.

This edition published by
The Orion Publishing Group Ltd
Orion House
5 Upper St Martin's Lane
London WC2H 9EA

An Hachette UK company
A CIP catalogue record for this book is available from the British Library

ISBN 978 1 4719 0267 3

All characters and events in this publication are fictitious and any
resemblance to real people, living or dead, is purely coincidental.

No part of this publication may be reproduced, stored in a retrieval
system or transmitted in any form or by any means without the prior
permission in writing of the publisher, nor be otherwise circulated in any
form of binding or cover other than that in which it is published without
a similar condition, including this condition, being imposed on the
subsequent purchaser.

www.orionbooks.co.uk

I

THE STIPENDIARY MAGISTRATE wrapped up the Leon Crow case for delivery to the Assizes. The police did not oppose bail. They were not vindictive. Crow was an old man rich in property, and he loved his wealth too much to run away and leave it. His bail was fixed at a substantial sum, and he put up the money himself. He had to. Not one man among the millions of a great city and its environs would be surety for him.

After the summary trial, Detective Chief Inspector Martineau and Detective Sergeant Devery walked from the Magistrate's Court to the C.I.D. office. The case against Leon Crow, receiver of stolen property, was their particular pigeon.

'He'll get five years,' said Devery.

'I wouldn't be surprised,' his superior replied. 'And that's as it should be. It's taken us a longer time than that to nail him.'

'Well, we've got him right. It gives me great satisfaction to restrain the liberty of a man like that. I wonder how many years he's been swindling honest burglars.'

'Too many,' said Martineau.

They strolled on in the mild sunshine of an April morning, two very tall men. Devery was well-built, lithe, dark-haired and handsome. Martineau, older and more powerfully made, was moderately handsome, too, in the way that a head carved in granite may be handsome. And his surprisingly blond hair, greying at the temples, gave

1

him an appearance of somewhat rugged distinction. In good grey suits, and good felt hats carelessly worn, both men were dressed with the intention of being inconspicuous. But their profession had marked them. In stamp and style they were unmistakably policemen.

Devery had more to say about Leon Crow, but Martineau scarcely listened. Now that the Crow case was finished until the Assizes, he had other things on his mind. And one thing in particular. Last night a detective inspector of Headquarters C.I.D. had failed to report off duty. And this morning, when Court began, he had still been missing.

'I wonder what can have happened to old Mick,' he remarked, with a frown of concern.

'It's a rum do, sir,' the young sergeant answered. 'But I don't think we need worry. The job he's on doesn't warrant any rough stuff.'

That was true. Inspector Robert McQuade, naturally nicknamed "Mick" after the famous brand of tobacco, was engaged in the prosaic business of unearthing evidence in the case of a swindling stockbroker. Hailing from Liverpool, and belonging in fact to that race of people known as the Liverpool Irish, he was a brilliant policeman of varied and sometimes unsuspected talents. He had, among other things, a qualification in accountancy. He was the obvious man to take on the stockbroker, who was proving himself to be a very slippery client. Very slippery, but physically harmless. It was hardly probable that McQuade had come to harm following the path of duty.

Still, McQuade was missing. He had not been home all night. His daughter, who had kept house for him since the death of her mother, was reported to be "in a state." Martineau had known McQuade for a very long time, and he liked him a lot. He was really worried.

In the Criminal Investigation Department Martineau went to his own office. He sat down at his desk and wondered if Detective Chief Superintendent Clay would

still be upstairs, making his daily report to the Chief
Constable. He buzzed the chief clerk on the intercom.

'Martineau here,' he said. 'Is Clay still up there ?'

'No, Harry, he isn't,' was the reply. 'He's just run
downstairs. There's hell on. They've found poor old Mick.'

Martineau's heart turned over. 'Where ?' he wanted to
know.

'In the river. He's at the mortuary now.'

'What's the cause of death ? Drowning ?'

'I don't know. I only got half the tale. There's a devil
of a flap on.'

'Thanks, Bert,' said Martineau. He rang off, and no
sooner had he done so than the intercom buzzed again.

'Martineau,' Clay's voice rasped. 'I want you. NOW !'

'Yessir. Right away,' said the chief inspector.

He pushed back his chair and reached for his hat. As
he strode through the long main office of the C.I.D., men
raised their eyes from their work and looked at him expectantly. They knew that something was in the wind,
and Martineau was the man for storms. This man had a
reputation, even among hardened policemen. He was direct
in nature and action, and his level glance showed it. But he
was direct without being naive. The cunning of an ex-
perienced detective is the cunning of a thousand criminals.
That direct glance of Martineau's could peel away pretence
like a surgeon's knife seeking the way to malignancy.

He knocked and entered Clay's office. He found the
C.I.D. chief pacing about, not in thought but in sheer
agitation. Clay turned at his entry, and his eyes were wild.
He was furiously angry, and deeply hurt.

'There's a car waiting,' he said. 'Have you heard ?'

Martineau nodded, and turned to the door. The two
men left the building, the stout superintendent stepping
out to match his subordinate's long stride. No further
words were spoken until they were in the car, and then
Martineau said quietly, 'I don't know any details.'

3

Clay emitted a heartbroken snort. 'Shot,' he said. 'Shot and dumped in the river. And somebody did a Gutteridge on him.'

Martineau was appalled. The classic case of Police Constable Gutteridge is still remembered in England. It embodies the application of criminal superstition ; savage superstition based on the uneasy belief that a murdered man's eyes retain after death the image of the last thing he saw, the face of his killer. The man who murdered P.C. Gutteridge afterwards shot out his eyes.

'He'll be a mess,' Clay went on. 'You and I will have to do the official identification of the body. We can't let that daughter of his see him with half his head blown off.'

Martineau did not reply because, at the moment, there was nothing to be said. His mind was busy scanning a mental picture gallery of the faces of people who might have cause or desire to kill Mick McQuade. He saw no likely suspect. As a detective McQuade naturally had had enemies in those shady regions which men call the underworld, but Martineau could think of no enemy who would take such a drastic vengeance. So far as he knew, nobody hated McQuade enough to take the risk of killing him.

At the mortuary they saw McQuade's body. They looked at the powder-burned eye sockets, for eyes there were none. They talked with the police surgeon, who was certain of the cause of death but as yet uncertain of the time. McQuade had been shot through the heart, and he had been dead when the two bullets were fired into his eyes. 'Sometime yesterday, fairly late in the day,' the doctor concluded. 'I may be able to give you a more exact time after the post-mortem.'

The two policemen had expected him to say something like that. Because the body had been lying in cold river water, neither temperature nor *rigor* was a reliable guide for the doctor. After the police had discovered the time of McQuade's last meal, and after he had examined the contents of the stomach, it was probable that he would be able to give a more accurate estimate of the hour of death.

Clay gave instructions for McQuade's clothes to be sent to the forensic laboratory. He watched Martineau gather together the contents of the pockets, then he turned away with a sigh.

'Nothing more to do here,' he said. 'We'll go back to the office and see if we can fill in the poor man's day for him. We might find something that way.'

'You know what's missing from this lot, don't you ?' said Martineau.

'I know. His official pocket-book. The murderer has seen that off, just to make it harder for us. We'll have to go back to his last report, and start from there. A job for you, Martineau.'

'You're giving me the case, sir ?'

'Of course. You're—you're not busy with anything else, are you ?'

He had been about to say that Martineau was the best man he had. He had refrained. He seldom praised a man to his face.

'Thank you, sir,' said Martineau. If he had been the sort of man to make wild statements, he would have said that he would see McQuade's murderer hanged if he had to work on the job for the rest of his life. That certainly was his frame of mind. It was Clay's attitude, too. Each guessed what the other was thinking, but neither made any comment.

They returned to Headquarters, and Martineau set to work. He studied the bulky file relating to the case of John Bassey, the unjust stockbroker. There were many people involved in the case, and many statements had already been taken. Martineau called in Devery, and they perused the statements with the object of discovering the names of men and women from whom statements had not yet been taken.

Some of these would be people whom McQuade had interviewed on the day of the murder.

Lists of names were made, and the two men began to make inquiries by telephone. In two hours they had filled in McQuade's day until half-past six in the evening, but they could get no information about his movements after that time. The detective inspector's last interview had been with Bassey's accountant.

'Did he say where he was going after he left you ?' Martineau asked, over the phone.

'He did,' the accountant replied. 'He said he was going to get a sandwich in Ella's bar at the Northland Hotel. I asked him if it was the end of his day's work and he said, "No. Not quite".'

'Nothing more explicit than that ?'

'Nothing more. I got the impression that he wasn't a very voluble man.'

'No, he wasn't. More's the pity. If you remember anything at all, let me know, will you ?'

'I certainly will,' said the accountant with feeling. Apparently the news of McQuade's murder had shocked him.

Martineau phoned the Northland Hotel in Lacy Street, and spoke to Frank Horton, the manager.

'No,' said Horton. 'I don't remember seeing Mr. McQuade, but I'll speak to Mrs. Bowie. He usually goes into the lounge bar when he comes in here.'

'Put Mrs. Bowie on, will you ?' Martineau asked.

'You want to speak to her yourself ? Certainly.'

A minute later Ella Bowie, the barmaid, came on to the phone.

'Hello, Ella,' the policeman said. 'I'm trying to find out where Mick McQuade was last night. Was he in your bar at all ?'

'I couldn't tell you, Mr. Martineau. I don't remember.'

'Now, Ella,' came the gentle rebuke. 'I don't think you're telling me the truth.'

'Why wouldn't I tell you the truth ? I can't be expected to remember all the fellows who come in here for a drink.'

'You rather liked McQuade, didn't you ?'

'What do you mean, "liked" ?'

'You'll get the details when you see your evening paper. He's dead, Ella. I'm not chasing him around for drinking on duty. I'm trying to find out who killed him.'

Ella's reaction to the news was normal for her. She was an attractive woman, but a tough one. She did not scream or express great horror. Martineau merely heard the quick catch of her breath, and then there was silence for a little while.

'I understand,' she said quietly. 'Yes, Mick came in here about six o'clock last night. He had a ham sandwich and a wedge of pork pie, and two glasses of beer. I don't think it was more than two.'

'Were you talking to him ?'

'For a minute or two. He said he was busy, so I guessed he was on duty. I said, "What poor fellow are you after now ?" and he said, "I'm not after a poor fellow, I'm after a rich fellow".'

'Did he mention any names, or any place ?'

'No. I thought he was gently pulling my leg, like he does—used to do. He was a good sort. Oh dear !'

Martineau thought he heard a sob.

'Yes, we'll all miss him,' he said. 'Did he say anything else ?'

'Not about where he was going, or who he was seeing.'

'No, I don't suppose he would. Did he seem to be worried or depressed about anything ?'

'No, he was just the same as usual.'

'Did he speak to anyone else in the bar ?'

'No. None of his friends were here.'

'How about enemies ? Were there any shady types in the bar ?'

'No. I'll tell you who they were.' She mentioned half-a-dozen names, and he wrote them down.

'How long did he stay ?' he asked.

'About half-an-hour.'

'Left at six-thirty. Thanks, Ella.'

'That's all right. Anything I get to know, I'll tell you.'

'Good girl. Cheerio.'

Martineau put down the telephone, and sat staring at his notes. He realized that he was at the beginning of a really difficult investigation. But there was no question of calling in Scotland Yard. Like a few more of the bigger police forces of England, Granchester City never asked for the Yard's murder specialists to be sent to their assistance. They had their own crack homicide men—of whom Martineau was one—and they had their own forensic laboratory. Moreover, their homicide men had one important qualification which a Scotland Yard man could not have in Granchester : a knowledge of the town and its criminals.

Martineau reflected that, so far, three little facts had been established. McQuade had taken food between six and six-thirty last night, he had been alive at six-thirty, and after that time he had intended to follow up some part of his inquiry. Well, that was a start. A start to a long, hard job. In the first place, every person connected with the Bassey case would have to be interrogated ; every person whom McQuade had interviewed, or had been about to interview. And yet, considering the nature of the Bassey case, it was very probable that the murderer had not the slightest connection with it.

Martineau picked up the telephone again, and began to make calls which would result in appointments. 'I'd better be having a look at some of these characters,' he murmured.

2

D URING THE FOLLOWING day, which was a Wednesday, Martineau and Sergeant Devery interviewed and eliminated from the McQuade job a number of people involved in the Bassey case. They saw perhaps one-third of the many people with whose money and shares Bassey had been juggling. Others they would see in due time. Some people were genuinely not available when they called, and some appeared to be wilfully elusive. Apparently these latter, for reasons of their own, did not wish to be brought into the case at all. Martineau ticked off their names with a grim smile. He reflected that they would evade him for a little time only. Eventually he would get around to them all.

Bassey himself had an unassailable and completely credible alibi. Moreover he was a middle-aged, flabby, irresolute man so cowed by the effect of the ruin he had wrought that it was almost impossible to imagine him committing or instigating any action so violent as murder by shooting. Neither did he have any discernible motive. Much of the evidence against him was already safely filed at Police Headquarters. The death of one investigating officer could not save him from the law's punishment.

That was Wednesday, a day of negative progress, and then on Thursday morning there was a happening which caused Martineau temporarily to forget the McQuade job. He received a call which sent him hurrying to the Granchester branch of the Northern Counties Bank, where he

9

had a small current account. The manager, a man he knew well, was waiting for him.

'One of the cashiers drew my attention to this,' he said. 'If he hadn't happened to know that you were a police officer, I don't suppose he would have bothered.'

"This" was a paying-in slip, crediting Martineau with fifty pounds. The signature at the foot of the slip was so badly written as to be almost undecipherable, but it could have been "L. Crow."

The manager went on : 'This fellow mentioned casually to the cashier that there was no need for you to be notified, because you were expecting the money. But yours being a vulnerable profession, I thought you'd better be told straight away.'

'You thought dead right,' said the policeman. 'When was the money paid in ?'

The bank manager was a small, stout man with a ruddy face and very shrewd eyes. The eyes were appraising Martineau coolly, and no doubt the brain behind them was wondering a little. 'About half-an-hour ago,' he replied.

'Well, I'm not expecting any money from anybody. This looks like some sort of plant. Can I see the cashier ?'

The manager nodded. He pressed a button on his desk, and a minute later a young bank clerk appeared. He was holding a bundle of notes in his hand. 'Yes, sir ?' he said. And, 'Good morning, Mr. Martineau.'

'A good morning to you,' said Martineau. 'And before we go any further, many thanks for drawing attention to this paying-in slip. Is that the money ?'

'Yes. I put it on one side, just in case.'

'Used one-pound notes, I see. Anything remarkable about them ?'

'No. They're perfectly good soiled notes. I haven't found any suspicious marks on them.'

'There won't be any. No point in it. Normally these notes would get lost among the rest of your takings. I don't think we need to examine the notes, but can you describe the man who handed them over ?'

'A scruffy old—a rather shabby, elderly man. Well turned sixty, I'd say. Small and thin, with grey hair and an unhealthy complexion.'

'A grey sort of complexion ?'

'That's right. And he had pinkish eyes. Pink-rimmed, I mean. And a long, thin nose. He reminded me of a grey ferret.'

'"That sounds like Leon Crow, all right," said Martineau, but he said it to himself. Aloud he asked, 'How was he dressed ?'

'A dark suit, shiny in places. And a bowler hat which was badly in need of brushing.'

Martineau made notes. 'Would you know him again ?'

'I certainly would.'

'Fine. Now I think I'd better have all this down on paper, while the going is good.'

He took a brief statement from the clerk, then he put his book in his pocket. 'I can't thank you enough,' he said. 'This could have been serious for me. Look after that paying-in slip, will you ? It might turn out to be Exhibit A.'

'I'll see to it myself,' said the manager.

'And mum's the word.'

'Oh certainly. We never talk about the affairs of our clients. You should know that.'

Martineau grinned and said, 'Sorry.' He left them then, and returned to Headquarters. He never used a typewriter, and he did not want any C.I.D. clerk to see the statement he had taken, so he made a copy of it in longhand and added his own report. With the documents in his hand he strode to Clay's office. 'Somebody's sniping at me,' he said.

Sitting as solid as a barrel behind his desk, Clay looked at the chief inspector, and at the papers in his hand. 'All right, what is it ?' he asked in his discouraging way.

Martineau gave him the papers, and he began to read.

'You're one of these strong, stylish and damned illegible writers,' he grumbled, but thereafter he was silent until he had read to the end.

'And I presume you weren't expecting this money ?' was his first comment.

'I certainly was not ! You should know me better than that.'

'Yes. And anyway you wouldn't be such a fool as to make any crook moves with Crow as your partner. He's trying to do you, right enough.'

'I don't see why. Crow wouldn't part with fifty quid just for the pleasure of seeing me get sent to gaol and lose my job. But how could he stand to gain ?'

'He could gain by discrediting the main police witness. And that could raise a suspicion in the minds of judge and jury that the whole of the police evidence is faked or exaggerated.'

'Even with Devery still giving evidence ?'

'I'm only stating a possibility. Or shall we say I'm trying to think the thoughts of Leon Crow. I'm not saying that it would actually turn out that way.'

'But all the evidence is in. There is no more to come. So, even if I were a bribe-taker, for what purpose could Crow be bribing me ?'

'Couldn't there be a made-up tale about new evidence ? Crow could say you went to him and told him what this new evidence was, telling him at the same time that it would put a year or two on his sentence. He could allege that you had undertaken to forget about this new evidence for a consideration. For two instalments of fifty pounds, say.'

'And let him put it in my bank account ? I'd be a mug !'

'And who would there be to come forward and give evidence that you were not such a mug ? Crow could say that he insisted on that sort of transaction as some sort of security for himself.'

'You're beginning to convince me. When asked about this so-called new evidence he could refuse to answer the question, on the grounds that such an answer would incriminate him. That refusal would strengthen his case against me, but it wouldn't make him any little white hen in the eyes of the judge.'

'Agreed. But that wouldn't mean much to him in his present position. He's trying to get away with the main job. He hasn't a cat-in-hell chance, but he probably thinks he has.'

'Happen he has a false witness or two. Against me.'

'Happen so.'

'The dirty little rat ! Ye gods, what's the world coming to ? There aren't any honest crooks nowadays.'

'It's fact. They'll do anything rather than take their medicine.'

'So what do we do ? Let Crow make his next move and then nail him ?'

Clay looked at Martineau. 'Do you want to be smeared?' he asked.

'Heaven bless all bank clerks. I have already reported the matter to the police authority. I'm in the clear.'

'That's what you think. Rumour is a dangerous thing. If Crow gets his squawk in, word might get around that he corrupted you, and that the Chief Constable and I rigged the job to clear you. You know what people are. It might be said that *we* also had a finger in the pie.'

'I can't credit that.'

'All right, look at it another way. It could be said that you arranged to accept the money, then got cold feet.'

Martineau sighed. 'You're right, of course,' he conceded. 'But I do hate to see Crow getting away with it. Maybe I'm prejudiced, but I think he should be punished in some way.'

Clay beamed craftily. 'You know how he likes money. I'm going to see that he doesn't get his fifty jimmy o'goblins back. That'll punish him plenty.'

Martineau grinned. 'Do I go and pull him in ?'

'You do not. You'll have nothing more to do with this. *I'll* send somebody to pick up Crow, and *I'll* talk to him.'

'Happen that would be wiser,' Martineau admitted.

'We're not going to waste a lot of time over this. We've got to clear the murder of one of our own men. You'd better go and be getting on with it.'

'Very good, sir,' said Martineau. He took his leave. On the way back to his own office he saw Devery working at a typewriter, catching up with the paper work arising from the previous day's inquiries. He remembered that Devery also was an important witness in the Crow case.

He stopped beside the sergeant. 'Do you have a bank account ?' he asked abruptly.

Devery was startled. He stared, and then he said, 'Yes, sir. For a bob or two. Nothing wonderful.'

'Which bank ?'

'Yorkshire Penny.'

'Nip round there straight away, and get to know the state of your account. If it's bigger than it ought to be, ask to see all recent paying-in slips.'

'Well, certainly. But why ?'

'Somebody might be trying to do you a thick 'un, that's why. You do as I say, and don't utter a word about it to anybody.'

'Very well, sir,' said the sergeant, still slightly be-wildered. His agile brain had not yet begun to guess at the reasons for Martineau's order. Later, but not much later, he would be extremely curious. He was a young man who liked to know what was going on.

14

3

IN THE INTERROGATION ROOM Superintendent Clay
sat and stared at a man whom he considered to be of the
lowest of a very low form of life. Not only was Leon Crow
a capitalist of crime and a receiver of goods well knowing
them to be stolen, he was a polluter and perverter of youth.
In his time he had tempted many a foolish young man to
begin a life of crime and vice. For years the patient police
had been stalking him. They had never doubted that they
would finally catch him, and now they had him.

The two men sat and faced each other across a bare
table. In a corner behind Crow a clerk sat at a small table,
waiting to take notes. A big detective stood with his back
to the door. They were the only people in the room, and
the tables and chairs were the only furniture. There were
no windows in the room, and the floor and walls were
bare except for two ventilators. A strong light shone down
upon the table in the middle, and it showed every line of
Crow's face. The "grill room" was a place to make a
suspect yearn desperately to see God's sunshine and the
free outdoors.

Clay stared for a little while longer. It was part of the
"treatment." The recipient of the stare began to shuffle
his feet uneasily on the concrete floor. Then Clay spoke.
'I suppose you know why you're here.'

The red-rimmed eyes were wary. 'I don't know a thing.
I'm waiting for you to tell me.'

Clay sighed heavily, and said, 'One thing I can't bear is corruption in a police force. When I find it in my own department I'll root it out, no matter who suffers.'

He paused, as if awaiting comment. But Crow said nothing. He watched, like a cornered rat watching a big dog.

Clay went on, 'That goes for the man who corrupts the policeman. He gets it in the neck, too, as far as I can give it. But the policeman comes first. He's betraying the entire force. There is absolutely no excuse for him.'

Again he paused, and still there was no comment, but the red eyes blinked under his hard glance. 'So,' he said slowly, 'I've got you, and I've got a man called Martineau. For what little service did you pay him fifty pounds ?'

Crow grinned nervously. 'It was a gift,' he said. 'I like Martineau. He's what I call an honest copper. He gave me a fair crack of the whip.'

'I daresay he did. He also nailed you proper. He's seen to it that you're going to get what's coming to you. You wouldn't give him fifty pounds for that.'

'And yet strangely enough I have given it to him.'

'You never gave away fifty pence in your life, never mind fifty pounds. Come on, why did you pay that money to Martineau.'

'I've told you already. It was a gift.'

'Did Martineau know you were going to put the money into his account ?'

'That's a difficult question to answer.'

'I'll bet it is. Answer it.'

'No. I'll have to have time to think about that one.'

'I think I know what you mean. You want to see how the job is going. Well, you won't have long to wait. Tell me this, would it hurt you to know that Martineau is not going to be allowed to keep your money ?'

Crow tried to seem indignant. 'Why can't he keep it ? It was my money and I gave it to him.'

'I'll tell you why. Except in very special circumstances, police officers are not allowed to accept gifts in money or in kind from members of the public. Martineau will have to return the money to you, or else he will have to hand it over to some approved charity. In the latter event your fifty pounds will have been wasted, from your point of view.'

'I'm no philanthropist. If Martineau can't keep it, I want my money back.'

It was Clay's turn to grin. 'I hope you get it.'

'Look here,' said Crow with sudden boldness. 'You tell me something for a change. How did you find out about the money so quickly ?'

'Easy. The bank notified Martineau. He got cold feet. He came to me and said he knew nothing about the money.'

'And do you believe that ?'

'I don't know what to believe. I'm just trying to get the truth of it. One thing seems fairly clear.'

'What's that ?'

'He intends to leave you holding the baby. He's backing out—if he ever was in.'

'And will he get away with it ?'

Clay shrugged. 'I suppose so. He came straight from the bank to me. Without other evidence, I don't see how we can get at him.'

There was a brief silence. Crow's eyes glittered with the intensity of his thoughts. He looked at Clay as if he were trying to read his mind.

'Are you trying to lead me up the garden ?' he asked suddenly.

'Certainly I am. Then, now, and all the time. But I'll tell you this straight. If I can't get you and I can't get Martineau, I'll see that I get your fifty pounds for charity.'

'What are you really after ?'

'I'm after seeing that a corrupt policeman goes out on

his ear—*if* he is corrupt. I'm also after seeing that you get punished in some way for bribing him or trying to bribe him.'

'And if I can prove that he got the money from me by a sort of threat, what then ?'

'Then you walk out of here, and you get your money back.'

'And Martineau ?'

'He gets the sack at the very least. It depends how strong the case is.'

Again Crow sat in desperate thought. Clay waited patiently. The trap was set ; the rat was sniffing at it.

Crow appeared to make up his mind. 'There *is* other evidence,' he said. 'Plenty of it, if you're prepared to believe me.'

'I wouldn't swing a cat on your unsupported word.'

'It isn't unsupported. I took precautions.'

'I'm glad to hear it. Tell me your tale.'

'Well, Martineau phoned me last night.'

'What time ?'

'Half-past ten. From a public call box.'

'How do you know that ?'

'I heard him press Button A.'

'All right. Go on.'

'He asked me if I was alone. I wasn't alone, but I said I was.'

'Why did you say that ?'

'I don't know. Caution, I suppose.'

'I get you. Continue.'

'He said he wanted to see me, right away. He said it was important, for me. I said I'd see him, and he said he'd be round in five minutes.'

'And was he ?'

'Less than five minutes. I only just managed to get my friends out of sight in time.'

'How many friends ?'

'Two.'

'A good thing they happened to be with you, wasn't it ?'

'It was. Martineau didn't give me time to arrange for anybody to be there.'

'No. It sounds as if he was taking reasonable precautions. What had he to say ?'

'He said he had some new evidence against me. He told me what it was.'

'What was it ?'

'You think I'd tell you ? Not likely !'

'All right. Go on.'

'He said that this new evidence would get me another couple of years, if it was submitted. He said that it *could* get mislaid.'

'If what ?'

'If I would contribute a hundred pounds to a police charity.'

'What police charity ?'

Crow grinned. 'The Inspector Martineau Benevolent Fund.'

'I see. And did you agree ?'

'No. A hundred nicker is a lot of lolly. But I did agree to give him fifty. He wanted it in one-pound notes, and he wouldn't give me a receipt. I baulked at that. I told him, "You think you can just come here and walk away with fifty jimmies, and me without a bit of proof you've got it ? Do you think I fell off a flitting, or summat ?" He said well that was the way it had to be, and I said not bloody likely. But we eventually settled that I should pay it into his bank account. He was a fool to agree to that, but I expect he wanted the money.'

'And your friends were listening all the time ?'

'Yes, behind the kitchen door. They heard every word.'

'Who are they ?'

'Aha. They're *my* couple of aces. I'll produce them when the time comes.'

'Both men of upright character, are they ? A couple of aldermen, maybe ?'

'Not quite that. But they'll do.'

'You know what this means, don't you ? Your refusal to give the names of witnesses here and now leads to the natural conclusion that you haven't any witnesses, and that you need time to find some. It also leads to the conclusion that the sort of witnesses you'll find won't be worth a tuppenny damn, anyway. It won't do.'

'All right, I'll tell you their names. Vincent Leary and Amos Gee.'

'A couple of tea-leaves !' Clay scoffed. 'Those two couldn't tell the truth if their lives depended on it.'

'Every man tells the truth at some time in his life. This is their time. They're ready and willing.'

Clay pretended to become thoughtful. He pondered. 'Assuming that they *are* telling the truth, your witnesses aren't so good,' he said. 'They both have records as long as York Road. If we go all the way against Martineau his counsel will make mincemeat of both of them. He might get away with it.'

'So, what is likely to happen ?'

'Full inquiries will be made. If there is a case against Martineau, we have three alternatives. We can make him stand trial and perhaps go to gaol. But that would be very bad for the reputation of the force and, as I said, he might get away with it. The other two possibilities are dismissal from the force or resignation as an alternative to dismissal. Either of those would be heavy punishment for a man of Martineau's rank and service. Also, we would be rid of a venal officer, and there would be no public scandal.'

'I suppose that would be better for everybody,' said the little fence mildly.

Clay regarded him grimly. 'Better for you, you mean. You'd get out of the job scot-free.'

Crow nodded coolly. 'And I'd get my money back. You'd make him restore it to me.'

'Happen,' said Clay. 'And happen not.' He turned to the others in the room. They had already been warned that the matter was absolutely confidential, and such a warning from a man with Clay's power in the force was sufficient to ensure their silence. To the clerk he said, 'All right, go and type it out.' To the detective he said, 'Get some paper and write down what you can remember of the interview you've just heard. You can do it in the waiting room.' To Leon Crow he said, 'You will sit in the waiting room until I've made one or two more enquiries. This officer will sit with you—just to make sure you don't steal the radiator.'

The last remark startled Crow. It was as if a stolid old bulldog had suddenly shown his teeth. His eyes glittered as he looked at Clay. His sudden uneasy doubt was visible, his thought obvious : Had he been led up the garden path, after all ? Had this stout, blunt-spoken old policeman made a mug of Leon Crow ?

'Come on, you,' said the detective, moving across the room with a suggestion of menace.

Crow rose hurriedly, and went out with the officer. Clay remained in thought for a little while, then he got up and followed. In the C.I.D. he encountered the detective inspector on duty.

'I want Vince Leary and Amos Gee, for interrogation,' he growled. 'Suspicion of conspiracy, if they try to be awkward.'

'Certainly, sir, I'll see to it,' said the inspector, as if it were simply a matter of sending out for two cups of tea.

One hour later, Amos Gee sat waiting in the police station, wondering which of his recent crimes had been traced home to him. Half-an-hour after that, Vincent Leary

21

was brought in, in a similar state of apprehension. When the two men saw each other, their doubts were resolved. They knew what it was all about.

Clay was so confident of his ability to handle these two men that he did not trouble to interview them separately, nor did he trouble to take them into the interrogation room. He had them brought into his office, and he sat frowning at them as they stood before his desk. The men were notorious petty thieves. They were the scum of their own degraded world. They had not the intelligence to devise a plan for an important crime, and they had not the nerve to commit such a crime even if they had had the intelligence.

Clay did not waste much time. 'We've got Leon Crow inside,' he began, with all the complacence of authority. 'He's been trying to make trouble for Chief Inspector Martineau, but he didn't get very far with it. We nailed him as soon as he tried to slip money into Martineau's bank account. Now he's trying to bring you two beauties into it.'

He paused, allowing Leary and Gee to see the situation as he wanted them to see it. Then he went on, 'I don't need to point out to you the seriousness of the offences involved. As you know, Crow's trial at the Assizes is pending, and Martineau is the chief witness against him. Conspiring to pervert the due course of justice is a very serious offence. Subornation or perjury is a very serious offence. Perjury, also, if it should come to that, is a *very* serious offence. In fact, I'd say that bearing false witness against a man like Martineau is damned dangerous. You know what he is.'

They knew what Martineau was. Their faces showed it. They were unnerved. This sudden pounce by the police, so soon after advance payment for a simple job of perjury had been made, was perhaps enough to upset anybody. But they were unaccustomed to believing anything told

22

to them by a policeman. They distrusted the police. Moreover, they had been warned by Crow that some policeman
would try to frighten them away. Now, when the thing
had happened, Leary at any rate had sufficient presence
of mind to try to find out exactly how strong the police
position was.

'Nobody can prove I've conspired against anybody,' he
said.

Clay smiled. 'Not yet,' he said. 'But when you give
evidence, somebody will. It's so simple I could cry over it.
Listen, I'll tell you exactly what will happen. First we have
Crow's tale. Martineau demands money for suppressing
some new evidence. Crow is not obliged to say what this
new evidence is, because the answer would incriminate him.
Therefore he thinks he has a strong case, because he has
two witnesses, all ready sweetened and briefed. Lovely.
Except that he's forgotten one thing. This so-called new
evidence. His witnesses are supposed to have heard the
entire conversation, so they know what the evidence is, if
there is any evidence. And they aren't quite as happily
situated as Crow. They can't refuse to answer the question
on the grounds that it would incriminate them. They can
only refuse an answer because they don't know any answer,
because there isn't any answer. And that's how they'll find
themselves up a gum tree. Oh, dear ! Two men with long,
long records as well. It's dreadful to think of what would
happen.'

Gee made his mind up quickly. 'I don't know what
you're talking about,' he said. 'I haven't seen Leon Crow
in a month of Sundays.'

'Can you prove that you weren't in Crow's house
between ten-thirty and eleven last night ?' Clay demanded.

'Yes, I can. I was in the taproom at the Prodigal Son.'

'And I was with him,' said Leary. 'And we were talking
to Doug Savage and his mother. Doug will remember,
because I had words with him about drinking up and

going home. They want you out of the place as soon as they've got your money, that lot do.'

'Joe Smithson was there,' said Gee. 'And Bert Teal, and Albert Berry. They'll remember.'

Clay wrote down names. He spoke into the intercom, sending out men to get statements from the people named. He sent for a clerk to get statements from Leary and Gee. And so, due to the overlooked defect which can often occur in a made-up tale and never in a true one, the conspiracy against Martineau was killed at birth, and Leon Crow was left at the mercy of Superintendent Clay.

While statements were being taken, Clay went to see the Chief Constable. His case against Crow was so "right", that he was afraid the Chief would want to prosecute the man. Nevertheless, the Chief would have to be told. Whatever the police did with Crow, it would have to be done on the Chief's instructions.

Clay was admitted to the great man's presence, and told to take a seat. The Chief, an alert, soldierly, rather impetuous man, asked him what he wanted. He told the story of Martineau, Crow, Leary and Gee in its entirety.

'Well,' said the Chief bluntly. 'It seems to be a straight up-and-down job. So why come to me ?'

'I was of the impression that you did not like this sort of thing to get into court, sir.'

'Your impression was right. Cases of that sort never do the force any good. They always leave a smear. But I can't see that we have any option about proceeding against Crow. If we didn't, I should think we would be compounding a felony.'

Clay coughed. The Chief glared at him. He had heard that cough before. 'Well, what is it ?' he snapped.

'Conspiracy is a misdemeanour, sir.'

'All right then, we'd be compounding a misdemeanour.'

'In the case of a misdemeanour, we can stifle a prosecution in the personal interest of the injured person.'

'Oh, can we ?' The Chief became thoughtful. 'We want to spare Martineau any embarrassment we can,' he said. He rose and went to his bookcase. He returned with a copy of Harris and Wilshere. In spite of his many years in high office, he had never forgotten that he was still a policeman. A policeman must take no man's word without verification, if verification is possible. He looked up Conspiracy, and he looked up Misprision and Compounding Offences. He put the book down.

'All right,' he said. 'What do you propose to do with Crow ? Put him through the wringer and let him go ?'

'Yes, sir. But we can also punish him by keeping his fifty pounds.'

The Chief stared. 'How ?'

'You could give Martineau official permission to retain the money which has been put into his account, and Martineau could donate it to the Northern Police Orphanage.'

'No !' said the Chief violently. 'That stinks of extortion. It would look as if we were letting him go for a consideration of fifty pounds. Either we proceed against Crow, or we give him a wigging and send him home. In either event we return his money.'

Clay bowed to authority. 'Very good, sir,' he said, showing none of his disappointment. 'Which shall it be ?'

'It seems a pity to let the man get off entirely, but we don't really want a prosecution. The satisfaction of seeing such a man punished would not offset the embarrassment to Martineau and to the force as a whole. There would always be people who would say that Martineau agreed to accept a bribe and then changed his mind. When you have got the job cleared and properly in order, you had better censure Crow and let him go. Talk to the man in a way he won't forget.'

Upon that tacit dismissal Clay rose. He took a small

liberty. 'Sir,' he said. 'I'll make him sweat. I'll put the wind up him properly.'

The Chief smiled, and that was the end of the interview.

Downstairs in his office, Clay went on with routine work until all the statements relating to the conspiracy had been brought to him. Then he had Leon Crow taken back to the interrogation room. Armed with copies of all the statements, he joined him there. Without a word he put the statements down in front of the little fence and went out again. He returned as the last statement was being perused.

He sat down, and watched. When Crow had read the statement he remained staring at it with unfocused eyes, looking inward at his own predicament. 'So they've let me down,' he said at last, almost to himself.

Clay did not trouble to inform him that his own faulty reasoning had let him down. He merely said, 'What else could you expect from two such characters ?'

Anger gleamed in the little red eyes. 'Well, I can soon let *them* down,' he shrilled. 'Those two shops in Richard Street, about a fortnight ago. Leary and Gee did 'em. They sold the stuff in Liverpool.'

Clay observed that the clerk in the corner was taking notes. 'Who bought the stuff ?' he asked.

'I don't know. I wouldn't tell you if I did know. It's those two I'm getting at.'

Clay reflected that the police were not going to come empty-handed out of the affair after all. 'What else can you tell me about them ?' he wanted to know.

Crow shook his head, and the superintendent guessed that he dared not disclose more about the two men because such disclosure would lead to his own involvement.

'I don't need to tell you how deep in the mire you are,' Clay said. 'But I can tell you how I can help you if you'll make it worth my while.'

'But how can you help me ?'

Clay fibbed. 'I told you the Chief didn't like the stink

26

of corruption. He's left it to me to decide whether or not we prosecute you.'

'And how can I make it worth your while *not* to prosecute ?'

'Information. You know what's going on, and I've got plenty of uncleared crimes.'

Crow was bitter. 'I sing for you, and then I get carved up by the boys.'

'My heart aches for you. And so does my foot. You know perfectly well that the police never disclose a source of information.'

'You're kidding again. I don't believe you can help me.'

'Well, I can't put it into writing for you. You'll have to take my word for it.'

'You'll really let me go if I give you the info about a few jobs ?'

'If it's good information, yes.'

Crow ferreted in the garbage pit of his mind. 'You remember that million-pound fire at Granchester Textiles last year ?' he began.

'Certainly I remember it.'

'Well, it was an arson job.'

Clay was startled. 'You're sure ?'

'I'm sure, because I know somebody who got a rake-off of the candle money.'

'Who was it ?'

'It was a certain person who'd be very dangerous to talk about. Very dangerous man. Mobster. I daren't mention the name.'

'Well, I dare. Do you mean Dixie Costello ?'

Crow closed one eye. 'I tell you I daren't mention the name,' he said.

'All right. But can you tell me how I'm going to prove anything against this certain person ?'

'No. I'm just giving you the tip.'

'Well, the tip is no good. The firemen and the insurance investigators found no evidence of arson after that fire. The inquiry was closed. I'm not going to open it again and burden myself with a case of arson just because of a draught of wind from you.'

'You wanted information, didn't you ?'

'I want something better than that. I want to know about the crimes on my books, the stuff I've got to clear. Come on, talk. And if you can tell me something really good about Dixie Costello I'll give you a bonus. I'll get you your fifty quid back.'

Crow brightened at the mention of the fifty pounds, but he could not nor would not give the information which would lead to the arrest of Costello. However, he did start to "sing," and once started he seemed to revel in betrayal. Then suddenly he stopped in the middle of a sentence, having nearly betrayed himself.

'Go on,' said Clay, deeply interested.

Crow shook his head. 'I can't tell you anything else,' he said.

The superintendent was well satisfied. His knowledge of the criminals and the crimes mentioned told him that Crow was not trying to fool him. When the information had been sifted, and acted upon, it would give quite a boost to the Granchester City Police average of crimes cleared. Crow had not been censured ; he had been pumped instead. The Chief would be pleased about that.

He brought out cigarettes and threw one on the table in front of Crow. He gave the man a light. 'Well, you're clear,' he said. 'We won't prosecute. And you'll get your fifty back, I'm afraid.'

'Is that a promise ?' Crow demanded, cheerful now.

'Yes,' said Clay. 'It wouldn't do for the police to have your money.' He looked curiously at the little man. 'It beats me. A man who loves money as much as you do, risking fifty smackers on the dumbest trick I ever heard of. You had a very slim chance of getting away with it, and you wouldn't have reaped much benefit anyway. I always thought you were a shrewd man.'

Crow's pride was touched. 'There aren't many shrewder in this town.'

'Only about a million.'

'That's what you think. If I told you the whole story about this, you wouldn't believe it.'

'Try me and see.'

'Gad, I think I will tell you. And I'll lay any money you don't believe me. I was paid to put that money in Martineau's account.'

'Who paid you ?'

'I can't tell you, because I don't know. I really haven't the faintest idea.'

'You don't expect me to believe that, do you ?'

Crow grinned. 'There you are. I said you wouldn't believe it. But it's true. A fellow phoned me. He talked as if he had a toffee in his mouth, disguising his voice very likely. He told me what to do. He was going to send me three hundred quid if I agreed. I was to follow Martineau, or have him followed, so's I could select two occasions when he didn't have an alibi. Then I was to get two witnesses so's I could tell the tale about Martineau demanding money. Then I was to put a hundred nicker into Martineau's account, and sign it with my own name.'

'A *hundred* pounds !'

'Yes. The fellow said if I did the job right it might help my case at the Assizes. But the main thing in his idea was to get Martineau sacked from the police.'

'And you agreed ?'

'Yes. I thought I'd got hold of a mug. I was going to get the money and do nothing. He'd never know. He'd have to believe what I told him. Anyway, the money arrived. It was stuffed into a big envelope and pushed through my letter-box during the night. There was a note

29

with it, written in block letters on a bit of toilet paper. It said if I didn't keep my bargain the writer would have me killed.'

'*Have* you killed ?'

'Yes. That's the bit I didn't like. It sounded like mob talk. And a mobster who can afford to part with three hundred quid just to get a copper sacked must be a middling big din. So I obeyed orders.'

'Except that you got your figures wrong.'

'Well, I thought fifty would sack Martineau just as easy as a hundred. I kept the other fifty for incidental expenses.'

The superintendent looked at Crow thoughtfully. The little man had the air of one who waits for applause after the performance of a parlour trick. If he had had a tail, he would have wagged it.

'You have an imagination, but not a brilliant imagination,' said Clay. 'I never heard so much cock-and-bull in my life.'

Crow was not abashed. He shrugged.

'Motive is what bothers me,' the superintendent went on. 'What was your motive in reciting all that twaddle ? What did you think it would get you ? Were you trying to put yourself right with me, or what ?'

'I guess I just got talking. Unburdening myself, like. I was that relieved when you said you'd let me go.'

Clay suddenly went red in the face. He jumped to his feet, and the other man cowered.

'Play the fool with me, will you ?' the angry man thundered. 'I said I'd let you go, so go ! If you aren't out of my sight in five seconds I'm liable to change my mind.'

Crow went. He departed in such haste that he left his bowler hat behind. He never returned for it.

4

WHEN MARTINEAU LEARNED how Clay had cleared him of the stigma of corruption, he was inclined to be amused by Leon Crow's story of an anonymous enemy who wanted him to be dismissed from the force.

'I wonder how he came to dream that one up,' he commented. 'On the spur of the moment, too.'

'It's the why of it which bothers me,' Clay replied.

'Yes, it does seem to be a bit motiveless. But he's a born liar, and happen he had been thinking that it would be a nice thing to ruin me with somebody else's money.'

'Maybe you're right,' the superintendent said. 'What a specimen. He's the complete fence, one hundred per cent rotten.'

Relieved of a small worry, Martineau went about his business, and he did not think of the matter again until he and Devery finished work—a cessation which was four hours overdue—at ten o'clock that night.

'I looked at my bank account like you said,' Devery told him. 'It was nearly ten pounds less than I thought it was.'

'Ah, mine was fifty pounds more,' he said. And because the young detective sergeant was one of the few men he trusted, and also had been his main helper in the Crow case, he told the story of the abortive conspiracy.

While he talked, the two men walked away from the

police station, cutting through narrow streets towards Lacy Street, a main thoroughfare. These old streets in the heart of the city were thronged with busy men in the daytime, but in the evenings they were mainly deserted. There were not even street girls to fade away at the approach of two men who looked like detectives.

When he had heard the tale, Devery made no immediate comment, and Martineau asked, 'Are you going to join me in a drink ? I think we've earned it.'

'Oh sure,' said Devery absently.

'Where ? The Northland ?'

The name banished the sergeant's pensive mood. 'I—I don't much care for the beer at the Northland,' he said.

'You mean you don't much care for the barmaid,' Martineau retorted in perfect friendliness. 'Are you scared of her, or something ?'

'No,' was the reply, and that was all.

They sauntered on. Martineau pondered. Ever since the nine days' wonder which the police remembered as the Plumber job, Devery had declined to enter the Northland Hotel, and Martineau had come to the conclusion that he was avoiding a meeting with Ella Bowie. Ella's estranged husband had been Caps Bowie, a member of the Plumber's gang. On the wild night which had ended the Plumber's career, Caps had been shot dead by Ella. Justifiable homicide, Martineau remembered. It had been a clear case of self-defence. But since then Devery had kept away from Ella's bar, and Martineau suspected that there had been something between them at the time of the killing. It was none of his business, of course. Devery was an unmarried man, anyway. Still, it was odd. He had a natural curiosity about it.

'Give the girl a break,' he said. 'She saved the hangman a job when she shot Caps.'

Devery made no comment about that, but he did say, 'All right, we'll go to the Northland if you like.'

So, to the Northland they went. The small lounge bar, more commonly known as Ella's bar, was well filled for the last half-hour of legal drinking time. Ella and another barmaid were very busy, but in spite of this Ella saw them as soon as they entered. When they found a place at the bar she came to them, a handsome and magnetically attractive woman of thirty with a scarred face. The scar had been made with a razor, when Caps Bowie had slashed her in a fit of baseless jealousy. The scar marred her only a little, and indeed some people thought that it gave her a more interesting appearance. Certainly it did not detract from the elemental appeal of her; but she was always aware of it, and she habitually kept the scarred side of her face turned away from people as much as possible.

Martineau thought that she looked rather pale, and he also thought that her eyes sought Devery's face rather hungrily. Nevertheless, she gave both men the same smile and word of greeting, and it was as casual as if she had last seen Devery twelve hours instead of twelve months ago.

She served them and left them, being obviously too busy to stay and talk, but neither of them had any doubts that she would return to them as soon as she had ceased to serve drinks at half-past ten. Each man took a long and grateful drink from his pint of bitter, and there was a short silence before Devery turned his eyes and his thoughts from Ella and brought up the matter which had been on his mind before.

'That business of old Crow is very queer, you know,' he said. 'He's no fool. There's only one thing that makes sense of it.'

'And what's that ?'

'His tale about the three hundred pounds shoved through the letter-box.'

'You think that makes sense of it ? I think it makes

it crazy. It was a damfool business to start with, but that tale—if we believe it—makes it worse.'

'There's one thing about it which rings true, and I can't see Crow being subtle enough to invent it.'

'And that is ?'

'He was told to pay a hundred into your account, and he only paid in fifty.'

'That was a mistake he made when he was spinning the yarn. He said a hundred and when Clay picked him up about it said he'd kept fifty for himself.'

'I don't think he could have made such a mistake. He was altogether too conscious of that fifty pounds.'

Martineau became thoughtful. Then he said, 'It defies credibility. Who on earth is going to put down three hundred of the best, on an extremely uncertain chance of getting me off the payroll ? Why, a man could have me murdered for a good deal less than that.'

'That is so. If I were you I'd watch my step.'

Martineau stared at his companion. 'You don't really mean that, do you ?'

'I'm not sure whether I do or not. Let us assume for a moment that Crow's tale is true. Somebody thinks you're on the Bassey case and wants you taken off it, or somebody knows you're on the McQuade case and wants you taken off that. This person has money, whoever he is. He reads the papers and he knows how Leon Crow is fixed. All these assumptions being correct, the conspiracy isn't as daft as it sounds. It could easily have resulted in your suspension from duty until after an inquiry. That would have resulted in the Bassey and McQuade cases being put into the hands of some other policeman. And maybe that's all the fellow wants.'

'You don't think this is a question of malice, then ?'

'I don't. Three hundred pounds' worth of malice ? No sir !'

Martineau was thoughtful now. He frowned into his

schooner of beer. He took a drink from it. At last he said, 'If Crow's tale is true, which I don't admit for a moment, then I must be a danger to somebody. Somebody wants me off the force because of something I know.'

'That seems to be about the size of it.'

'But what do I know that you don't know ? What do I know that isn't already reported and committed to police records ?'

'It may not be what you know, but whom you know.'

'Well, you and I have worked together now for quite a few years. Whom do I know that you don't know ? Professionally, I mean. Among the riff-raff and the rough-necks.'

'You can forget the riff-raff. Three hundred pounds, remember.'

'Oh, rubbish ! I can't see it. Leon Crow made it up, the old buzzard.'

Devery shrugged, refraining from further argument. They began to talk about something which seemed to Martineau to be vastly more important. The job in hand. The McQuade murder.

The two investigators had again spent most of the day interviewing people who were involved in the Bassey case, but they still had no trace of McQuade's movements after half-past six on Monday evening. Neither had anything been learned from the squad of plain clothes men who had been making inquiries along a much lower stratum of Granchester society, in what could be loosely called the underworld. Neither had anything been learned by the main body of the force, a thousand men with eyes and ears alert for the slightest clue or hint which might lead to elucidation of the McQuade problem. Neither had any information come in from other police districts ; and no unsolicited information of any value had come from the general public. 'We're getting nowhere fast,' Martineau commented.

'How many of the Bassey people have we to see yet ?' Devery wanted to know.

'About a dozen. The awkward squad. Away from home, too ill, too big and too busy, or deliberately elusive. And when we've seen them all we'll probably find we've been wasting our time. But see them we must.'

'And when we've seen them all ?'

'We'll be at a standstill. Murder without a clue. Clay has listed every crook that Mick ever sent down, and those who are still with us have been interviewed. He says none of them have the nerve or the means or the motive for the job. The trouble is that for a policeman Mick was a well-liked man. He was even moderately popular with crooks like Dixie Costello. He used to get more gratuitous information than any copper on the force. But his informers aren't ringing in with anything on *this* job, you'll notice. Not a murmur.'

'It's quite possible that Mick didn't have an appointment that evening. The man upon whom he intended to call may have been unaware of the intention.'

'If that man was the murderer, it's extremely likely. Hey, there's an idea ! Mick dropped in on an elusive client unexpectedly, and for some reason that person killed him.'

'Motive ?'

'We don't know, do we ? Mick might have found him doing something pretty seriously wrong, or he might have recognized him as somebody else entirely. For instance, some man wanted by the police, going under an assumed name.'

'Very nice, and quite possible,' Devery concurred. 'That makes it imperative that we should see every one of the Bassey lot.'

'It does indeed. And the ones who don't want us to see them, they're the fellows we're determined to see.'

'And to see them before they see us, if possible.'

'That's the idea, boy. We'll make a policeman of you yet.' Martineau finished his beer. 'Fill 'em up, Ella.'

At half-past ten Ella came to talk to them. 'How are you getting on with your case,' she asked Martineau.

'It's in the bag,' he told her gravely. 'At any moment we expect to make an arrest.'

She smiled drily. 'When I can get a word of truth out of you, that'll be the day.' She looked at Devery. 'It's been a year since I saw you. I'm out of mourning now.'

He was embarrassed. 'Why bring that up ?'

She shrugged. '*I'm* not afraid to talk about it.'

Martineau was watching too closely : Devery changed the subject. 'How are you, anyway, Ella ?' he asked.

'As well as could be expected. And you ?'

'Quite fit, thanks.'

'Good. And is the girl friend quite fit, too ?'

'No girl friend, Ella.'

'Except you,' said Martineau, with mischievous intent. Then he looked at his watch. 'Oy, I've got a bus to catch. Cheerio, Devery ! Be seeing you, Ella.'

'I must be off, too,' said Devery. 'Good night, Ella.'

'Good night,' she responded. 'And will you be seeing me, too ?'

He was turning away. 'Hard to say,' he replied.

Her glance followed him to the door. He may have been aware of it, but he did not turn his head. She sighed, and rather sadly she set about the business of gathering up empty glasses.

.　　　.　　　.　　　.　　　.

The following day, which was Friday and a good day because it was pay day, Martineau and Devery began work by listing the people concerned in the Bassey case who had not been reported as interviewed by Inspector McQuade. From this list Martineau ticked off the names of a number of people whom he had seen himself, and whom he considered to be the absolute last resort as murder suspects. The list was further curtailed by inquiry. One man was in South Africa and had been there for some time, another was very ill with thrombosis and had been in bed at the time of the murder, and another had retired and gone to live at Swanage, and so would have to be interviewed by the Dorsetshire County Police. Remaining on the list were seven men and a woman ; seven mystery men and Madame X. If Martineau's idea of the previous night did indeed turn out to be an accurate guess at the facts, then McQuade had walked in unexpectedly upon one of those eight people, and had been killed for his intrusion. Martineau still thought that such an event was not beyond the bounds of possibility.

The names on the list were : Eugene Drax, Lionel Hart, William Stanton Hope, Sylvia Paris, William Taylor, G. Llewellyn Thomas, Reuben George Walters, and Hubert Warren. Both investigators took note of the names, along with business and private addresses and telephone numbers.

'Now,' growled Martineau, 'you never know your luck. Go and see if any of these characters has a record. I'll see if I can contact Drax.'

Devery went to look at records. Martineau phoned the mid-town office of Drax and Weaver, chartered accountants. A girl with a pleasant voice told him that Mr. Drax had called in the office and this very minute had left for Scotland. Mr. Drax, it appeared, was going to spend the week-end trying to pull salmon out of the River Tweed. He would call at the office again some time on Monday afternoon. Martineau thanked the girl and then said something about Mr. Drax under his breath.

The next person on his list was Lionel Hart. Mr. Hart's business address had not been ascertained, but he lived at The Elms, Elms Road, Davidsham. Davidsham was an outlying suburb of the city, a good six miles from where

Martineau was sitting. He picked up the telephone again.

Again his call was answered by girl. A housemaid, he supposed. 'Could I speak to Mr. Hart ?' he asked.

'Mr. Hart is engaged with a visitor at the moment,' the girl said.

Martineau thought : Another brush-off. Aloud he said, 'This is Chief Inspector Martineau of the city police. Kindly put me through to Mr. Hart at once.'

'Yes sir,' said the girl breathlessly, and Martineau felt like a bully. He waited, and presently he heard a calm, well-modulated, quite friendly voice : 'Lionel Hart here. What can I do for Chief Inspector Martineau ?'

'Can we make an appointment ?' Martineau asked. 'I want to see you with regard to a matter connected with the Bassey case.'

'Why, certainly. But I'm afraid I can't see you this morning. I have to go into town.'

'Town is where I am. Could you spare a few minutes to call at Police Headquarters ?'

'Of course, yes. I never thought of that. What time do you want me to call ?'

'At your convenience, Mr. Hart, so long as you can give a time. When can you call ?'

'Ummm. I'll come to your place as soon as I get into town. Get it over, what ? Would half-past ten do ?'

'That will do fine. Just ask for me, I'll be waiting. Good-bye, Mr. Hart.'

'Well,' said Martineau as he put down the phone. 'He's saved us a trip into the backblocks, at any rate.'

'Who ?' asked Devery, who had just returned to the room.

'Lionel Hart. Did you find anything ?'

'No. None of those names in our records. Do we try Wakefield and Scotland Yard, just in case ?'

'We do,' said Martineau. 'See to it.'

Devery went out again. Martineau phoned the office of

William Stanton Hope, stockbroker. Once again he was answered by a girl. She said that she thought Mr. Hope was engaged with a visitor, and who was speaking ?

Martineau told her. He also announced uncompromisingly that he would hold the line until Mr. Hope was *not* engaged. 'Yes, sir,' the girl said.

He waited. Five minutes later the girl spoke to him. 'I'm sorry,' she said timidly. 'Mr. Hope has had to go out. Can you give me your number and he'll call you when he comes in ?'

Martineau was angry. Four times in three days William Stanton Hope had avoided an interview. But the words which arose in Martineau was not heard by the girl. He gave his number and rang off, and then he took his pencil and heavily underscored the name of Hope. 'I shall certainly be seeing *you*, brother,' he muttered.

He called the home of Mrs. Sylvia Paris, and again the answer came in a feminine voice. 'Mrs. Paris ?' he asked hopefully.

'No, sir,' the woman replied. 'I'm the cleanin' lady. Mrs. Paris has just gone out.'

Martineau left no message. He dialled the business number of William Taylor, and while he was doing so Devery returned and perched on the corner of the desk.

The inevitable girlish voice informed Martineau that Mr. Taylor had gone to London. He would not be in the office until Monday morning.

The inspector sighed, and tried G. Llewellyn Thomas. To his surprise he was able to speak to G. Llewellyn, and furthermore the gentleman agreed to see him that afternoon. Encouraged, he went after Reuben George Walters and Hubert Warren, and they also agreed to see him during the afternoon.

'Not so bad,' he commented when he finally put down the telephone. 'That'll only leave four. Drax, Hope, Mrs. Paris, and Taylor. And Hope's the boy we'll see first.'

He looked at his watch. Lionel Hart was due in fifteen minutes. 'Just time for us to go and draw our pay and have a quick coffee in the canteen,' he said.

5

LIONEL HART was punctual. At precisely half-past ten he was ushered into Martineau's office. He was tall, spare, and grey-haired. He appeared to be about sixty years old, but his lined, aquiline face was still handsome. He was well-dressed, and moreover completely dressed, with hat, stick, gloves and a flower in his lapel. His perfunctory handshake was easy and sure. Obviously he was used to meeting people, and he had the manner of a man who considers himself to be of no small importance.

Hart took the seat which was offered to him, a chair facing the window. He sat upright, with his stick between his knees and his hands clasped over the head of the stick. He did not wait for questions to come, but began briskly : 'About the Bassey affair, Inspector. There isn't a great deal I can tell you. I did do a certain amount of business with the man at one time, but it was all quite satisfactory. He bought and sold for me quite according to instructions, and I never suspected that he wasn't as safe as the Bank of England. I suppose I was lucky. I have records of all the deals somewhere at home. You can see them if you like, but I don't think they'll help you much.'

'That's very good of you, Mr. Hart.' Martineau replied. 'I don't need your records myself, but the officer who takes over the Bassey investigation might like to see them.'

Hart was surprised. 'But you said you wanted to see me about the Bassey case.'

'With regard to a matter *connected* with the Bassey case. That was the late Inspector McQuade's last job. He was working on it the day he was murdered. *I* am investigating the murder.'

Hart was amazed. He went red in the face. He gobbled, and the two watching policemen perceived that he was not an eagle, but a turkey.

'But—but what am I supposed to know about the murder ?' he demanded.

'Well, you may know that it happened last Monday evening. Did you see Inspector McQuade on Monday evening ?'

'I most certainly did not !'

'Did you have an appointment to see him ?'

'No !'

'Did you see him on Monday at all ?'

'I did not. So far as I know, I never saw him in my life.'

'Now, Mr. Hart, don't take this matter to—— Don't take this matter too seriously. I'm not suggesting that you had anything to do with a murder. I'm just trying to fill in McQuade's day up to his death. Did you have a phone call from him on that day ?'

Hart calmed down. 'No, Inspector, I can't help you with that at all,' he said. 'I know nothing about Mr. McQuade's movements or proposed movements on Monday or any other day.'

'Thank you. Incidentally, just for the record, where were you on Monday evening ?'

'I was at home. I never went out. I didn't have any visitors either, come to think of it. But if you ring up my house, I daresay my housekeeper will be able to tell you where I was.'

'I may do that later. What is your profession, Mr. Hart?'

'I'm retired. I was a tea-planter. In Ceylon. I spent years out there.'

'And how long have you been retired ?'

'Oh, about twelve years.'

'What made you settle in Granchester ?'

'I tried Eastbourne and I tried Bournemouth. I never saw so many old folk in my life. Gone there to try and keep alive a bit longer, y'know. I felt I was in the presence of death all the time. Like a healthy graveyard, as what's-his-name said.'

'Still, sooty Granchester ?'

'I had friends here. Still have. It's a smoky hole, I know, but I like it. And of course I can afford to live out in the green belt.'

'And you interest yourself in stocks and shares as a hobby ?'

'That is correct. I try to make a bob or two.'

'Ah, we all like to do that. Well, I won't detain you any longer. Thank you for calling.'

'Don't mention it. Pleasure,' said Hart, rising immediately. 'Good morning to you. I can find my own way out.'

When Hart had gone, Martineau commented, 'He seems to be all right, at any rate.'

Devery agreed, then added rather wistfully, 'I was thinking about finger-prints, as a means of identification. If we could get the dabs of some of these people, we could soon find out if any of them have a record under another name.'

'Yes, but how to get them, that's the thing. They'd scream like hell if we asked them to ink their fingers.'

Again Devery agreed. 'I was watching Hart,' he said. 'He didn't touch a thing in this office except the knob of his swagger stick. I thought he might handle the door-knob as he went out, but he put his gloves on first.'

'Doorknob prints are never any good, anyway,' Martineau replied, and the topic of finger-prints was closed.

The chief inspector made a few notes, and then he said, 'Come on ; we'll see if we can find William Stanton Hope.'

They got their hats and they were on their way out of the building when Devery excused himself and went into the men's washroom. 'I'll catch you up, sir,' he said as he went.

Martineau nodded, and strolled out of the building. It was a fine, mild morning. Still strolling, he headed for the financial district which made busy those same narrow streets which he and Devery had found deserted the night before. There, besieged by banks and office buildings, and relieved by the nearness of a few small, select taverns and a couple of good restaurants, stood the Stock Exchange, Temple of Mammon and a place of occult rites where all activity could be stilled by the shouting of the mystic number "Fourteen hundred !" to denounce the presence of an intruder.

Thinking about the business in hand, Martineau went along until he came to a cross-roads about two hundred yards from Headquarters. The lights were in favour of the traffic which sped past him, and he had to wait. He turned and looked behind him, expecting to see Devery somewhere near. The sergeant was a hundred yards away, and when Martineau turned he began to behave in a peculiar manner. He signalled with the action of a man putting a pair of field-glasses to his eyes, and then he moved out of sight by dodging into the doorway of the nearest shop.

The lights changed, and Martineau crossed the street. Devery's signal meant that someone was watching him, and since he was walking it also probably meant that someone was following him. He had a shadow, and Devery, coming out of Headquarters a minute's slow-walking distance behind him, had naturally seen the shadow and was doing a little shadowing on his own account.

That being so, the thing for Martineau to do was to walk aimlessly for a little while, turning this way and that

45

but not too suspiciously often, to make sure that the shadowing business was not merely a matter of two men happening to go in the same direction. He turned aside, and sauntered along a short street which was lined by smart shops. The street took him into the main thoroughfare of Bishopsgate. He paused for a moment and looked at a display of garden furniture in the window of a department store, then he walked on. Soon he had left the district of the smartest shops behind, though he was still very much in the heart of the city. Ahead of him lay the cathedral, and two big railway stations, but he had no intention of walking so far. He had work to do, and not much time to waste on this creature who came slinking along behind him.

He saw the sort of street he needed for his purpose. It was a narrow street between the walls of factory yards. One of the walls was unbroken, the other had only one gateway, and that seldom used. It was a street which one would expect to be deserted for most of the day. He went along this street, and without looking back he entered the gateway. There he waited for one minute by his watch, and then he stepped out into the street. A man was coming towards him, and behind the man was Devery. Martineau knew the man well. His name was Bert Preston, and his criminal record was long and bad, though he was still a young man.

When Martineau emerged from the doorway, Preston turned to flee. He saw Devery, and knew that he was trapped. He waited, and the two policemen closed in on him.

'Now then, Bert, what's the gag?' Martineau asked pleasantly. 'I never knew you liked me enough to follow me around.'

'I weren't following you,' said Preston sullenly.

'You were. And you were ready to run until you saw there was a man behind you.'

'Even if I were following you, there's no law against it.'

'This time I'm going to be my own law, Bert. I wasn't inclined to believe that somebody is trying to get me into serious trouble, but now I've seen you operating, I'm sure of it. I want to give you the proper picture, Bert. Somebody is trying to get me sacked from the Force, and that somebody is paying you to report on my movements. I've got a wife and child, Bert, and if I get sacked from the Force they'll probably suffer more than I will. The very thought of that makes me mad, Bert. So now you'll tell me all about this man who's paying you, or I'll lame you. I mean I'll lame you.'

'You daren't do it,' Preston denied, but there was no confidence in his voice.

'I daren't *not* do it. Get that into your thick skull.'

Devery intervened. 'Let's not be brutal with the man, sir. We can put him out of the way with a lot less trouble than that. Let's take him in for loitering, and then find a twelve-inch jemmy in his pocket. With his record he'll get ten years' preventive detention for that.'

Martineau frowned, pretending to consider the idea. 'Generally speaking, I wouldn't do that to a dog,' he said. 'But I've got myself and my family to think of. All right. If he's one of the fellows who are plotting against me we'll take him in and do him.'

Preston was staring in terror. Preventive detention was the bogey of such men as he. 'You can't do it. It's a dirty fix,' he screamed.

'Hush, man, hush ! I might let you go if you tell me what I want to know. *Only* if you tell me what I want to know. Why are you following me ?'

'I don't know.'

'Oh, let's take him in,' said Devery, with impatient disgust.

'No, no ! It's the truth I'm telling you. An envelope was shoved through my letter-box. There was ten quid

47

in it, and a letter. It said I could earn ten quid a day by following you around and reporting every move you made. I was to make notes, like a proper diary. I was to keep these notes in my pocket till I got further instructions, which would come by post.'

Martineau and Devery exchanged glances. This was indeed support for Leon Crow's story.

'Somebody's a mug to trust you to follow me around all day,' the inspector remarked. 'In an hour or two you'd have been sitting in a taproom, resting your tired feet and making the diary up in your head.'

Preston shook his head seriously. 'In the letter it said another fellow would be on *my* tail,' he said. 'I didn't know but what that might be true. I did spot a bloke who might have been following me.'

'What sort of a bloke ?'

'A scruffy little corner boy. No hat and a right lot of black hair. Open-necked shirt and a black Teddy Boy suit what looked as if he'd slept in it for a year.'

'Have you got the letter with you ?'

Preston's hand went to his inside pocket. It came out holding a flimsy piece of paper. He passed the paper to Martineau. It was toilet paper, and its message was written in block letters, in pencil. Martineau read it, then carefully put the paper away between the leaves of his pocket book. 'I don't think that will tell us much,' he said.

'Are you going to let me go now ?' Preston wanted to know.

'Yes. And so long as this man keeps on giving you ten pounds a day, you can keep on following me. It's good pay and it will keep you out of mischief. By the way, where's the envelope ?'

'I chucked it in the fire.'

'A pity. Mind you don't chuck the next one into the fire. Now let me see the money.'

Preston was in agony again. 'You're not taking that !'

'You can keep it in your hand. I just want to see it.'

Reluctantly Preston delved into the fob pocket of his trousers and brought out a small wad of notes.

'Open it up,' said Martineau. 'I want to look at each single note, back and front.'

Preston did as he was told. Martineau scrutinized each note. As he had expected, there were ten well-used one-pound notes, with no marks upon them which should not have been there.

'All right,' he said. 'Now here's the drill, Bert. No harm is going to come to you. You just keep on with your assignment, and soon you might get another message, with instructions to report. That's when you phone the police station and contact me, or leave a message for me. I want to know exactly what instructions are given to you. Is that clear ?'

'Clear enough. And somebody might rub me out for it. For all I know I might be dealing with the real tigers.'

'Nobody will rub you out, Bert. Nobody will know. You'll call yourself Number Twelve when you ring in. You can't forget that number. One dozen. The first reserve. I won't mention your name to anybody, and neither will this officer. You'll be quite safe.'

'I don't like it,' said Preston.

'No, but you'll do it,' said Martineau coolly. 'You'll do it, or else I'll make you sorry you were born. You're damned lucky to be *allowed* to do it, after this morning's caper. Remember that. All right, we'll toddle along now, and you can follow at your leisure.'

They left the man then, and started to make their way to their original objective, Fitzwilliam Street, where William Stanton Hope had a suite of offices.

'Do you think he'll do it ?' queried Devery as they walked along.

'Who, Bert ? You think I was a bit soft with him ?'

49

'I'm inclined to think so. You didn't scare him enough. He may be more scared of the other party.'

'Maybe. We'll have to wait and see. It's a dicey job anyway. I think this bashful character who's trying to ruin me will take damn good care that Bert Preston doesn't lead us to him. We're just working on the long chance, that's all. It's what you've got to work on when there's nothing else.'

'If there's a second tail, the job's finished. Preston won't hear another word from Bashful, and he'll get no more ten quids.'

'That is so. We'll have to look out for Tail Number Two. He could even be heading us right now, though I've been looking and I haven't spotted him.'

They came to Fitzwilliam Street, which was quietly busy and restrainedly opulent after the manner of financial thoroughfares. They found W. S. Hope's office building, and from across the street they identified the office, which was on the third floor. There were six windows bearing the Hope name in gold lettering, indicating that the man owned or rented quite a large suite.

Martineau turned and looked at the building which faced Hope's place. 'I think we'll try and get a look at this fellow,' he said. 'Before we call, we'll make sure he's in.'

They walked along to the main entrance of the opposing building, and went inside. Facing them were stairs, and a lift. They went up the stairs, which made a squared spiral around the lift shaft. On every floor there was a landing, and every landing had a window which overlooked the street. From the window of the fourth floor landing they could look across the street, down into the offices of W. S. Hope.

They saw girls and men working, girls and men not working. The end office of all, directly opposite to them, seemed to be a very sumptuous place. In that room there were two men. One of them was sitting at a big desk and the other was in an armchair. Looking into the shadowed room, the two detectives could see the face of the man at the desk fairly clearly. But the man in the armchair was much further away from the window. They could not see his face at all, but they could make out his feet and his general attitude. His legs were outstretched ; his elbows and not his hands rested on the arms of the chair, and the angle of his body indicated that he was looking straight up at the window where the two detectives stood.

'Well, there you see William Stanton Hope, Esquire, the man who hasn't time to bother with such unimportant people as the police,' Martineau commented.

'They're having a bit of a session,' said Devery. 'Can you see the bottles on the desk ?'

'Yes, but I don't suppose I shall be looking at them for long. The chap in the armchair will be spotting us any minute now. Not that it matters.'

Martineau was wrong. Apparently it did matter to the man in the armchair. Suddenly this man stood up and retreated to the back of the room, where his figure was just faintly discernible to the men across the street. The man at the desk seemed to say something. There was a pause, then the man at the desk, tall, grey-haired, and distinguished in appearance, turned as if he would look out of the window. He changed his mind about that, perhaps after a word of warning from his companion. He resumed his former position, said something briefly, and then there was a change of light in the room as a door at the rear was opened and closed.

'That bird spotted us, and then beat it,' said Martineau. 'I wonder why. Come on !'

The two detectives raced down the stairs, and out into the street. 'Stay here and watch the front,' said Martineau. He looked rather hopelessly at the long block of offices. There seemed to be no way of getting round to the back for quite some distance. He crossed the street and entered the Hope building, and went straight through it in search of a back door. He found the door, and stepped out into a small backyard which was almost filled with rubbish bins. The backyard gave access to a narrow back street, and there was a short alley running through to a parallel street. He went through the alley, and found himself within ten yards of a busy shopping street. If the unidentified man had reached that street and joined the throng of people on the sidewalk, then he had got clean away.

Martineau returned to the Hope building. He found the back stairs, of uncarpeted stone and concrete, and climbed to the third floor. As he had expected, he found a narrow rear corridor which ran behind the Hope suite of offices. There were four doors on the corridor, all on the same side, and on the other side were windows. Martineau went along, cautiously trying the doors. The first three were secure, and they had the immovability of doors which are never used. The fourth door was marked "Strictly Private." He knocked.

The door was opened by the tall man whom Martineau had seen from the other side of the street. He stood blocking the doorway, though his stance and expression suggested complete confidence and calm. There was no hint of defensiveness about him.

'Good morning,' Martineau said.

'Good morning,' the man replied. 'This is a private entrance. People only come this way by invitation.'

'I see,' said the policeman coolly. 'I am Chief Inspector Martineau of the City Police. Are you William Stanton Hope ?'

'I am.'

'I would like to speak to you, indirectly, in regard to the Bassey case. I believe you were involved.'

'In a small way, in my capacity as a stockbroker.'

'Nevertheless, you were involved. But I'm not primarily

52

concerned with that. I'm more interested in your movements and appointments on Monday last. May I come in ?'

'Have you a warrant ?'

'No.'

'Did you come the back way so that my staff would
not see you ?'

'No.'

'Why did you come this way ?' Hope asked, but he
turned back into the room and indicated that Martineau
should enter.

'I'll explain in a little while,' said the big detective as
he stepped through the doorway. Hope stayed to close the
door, and the visitor had a second or two to look around
him without his curiosity being observed. He noticed par-
ticularly the bottles on the tray which stood on the corner
of the desk. Bollinger, Courvoisier, and White Horse.
Champagne—a half-bottle—brandy, and whisky. Hope
certainly treated his back-door visitors well. In addition
to the bottles there were a soda siphon, a pint-size silver
tankard, and an ordinary spirit glass. Martineau wondered
who had been drinking what. He had also heard of men
who drank champagne laced with brandy. There was a
name for that luxurious mixture. Now what was it ? He
couldn't remember.

Hope said, 'Will you sit down ?' and Martineau took
the armchair. He leaned back and looked up at the window
where he had so recently been standing. Yes, he thought,
the man in the armchair had spotted him, all right.

Hope sat down in the desk chair. 'You were saying ?'
he hinted with cold politeness.

'I wasn't saying anything,' said Martineau. 'But I would
like to talk about Inspector McQuade.'

'The inspector who was murdered ?'

'Yes. He was investigating the Bassey case. Did you
see him on Monday ?'

'No. I have never seen him.'

'Did *he* try to see *you* ?'

Hope pondered. 'Yes, I believe he phoned twice. But I was very busy. I did not get into contact with him.'

'You were very busy every time *I* tried to reach you, too, weren't you ?'

Hope smiled faintly. 'Yes, I'm afraid so.'

'Have you heard any of your business acquaintances speak of having seen McQuade ?'

'No. There's a lot of talk about the Bassey affair in financial circles, but not by the people involved. They're keeping quiet. Nobody knows where the job will finish, you see.'

'It'll finish in front of one of Her Majesty's judges. Who was the man who was in here a few minutes ago ?'

'I'm sorry. Certain clients like to see me in private. I respect their desire for privacy.'

'Mr. Hope, I am investigating a murder case.'

'And what connection can there be between your murder case and a man who happens to call privately at this office ?'

'There could be a connection.'

'How ?'

'I don't think it would be wise for me to tell you.'

'If you'll pardon a blunt observation, Inspector, I think this is a lot of nonsense. You don't seem to understand. Secrecy is sometimes important in the preliminary discussions of share transactions. I have a large staff, and one or two of them may not be as discreet as they ought to be. That is why a visitor may sometimes come and go by the back door. That back door is a very handy thing for me. It saves me the trouble of going to clients' houses for dinner, and that sort of thing.'

'You can trust the police not to be indiscreet about your clients. Who was the man ?'

'I can't tell you. He's got nothing to do with your murder, anyway.'

'He left in rather a hurry, didn't he ?'

'He did, rather. He remembered that he had another appointment. Did you see him go ?'

'I saw him go.'

'Then why didn't you stop him and ask him his name ?'

'I think you know why.'

'Are you one of the men who was looking into this office from across the street ?'

'I may be.'

'Not quite the thing, is it ? Spying on somebody.'

'It's quite the thing, all right. When you play the Elusive Pimpernel, Mr. Hope, you play the game your way. By doing so you make the police think that you might be worth a few minutes' observation. So they play the game their way. You brought it on yourself.'

'Perhaps you're right,' Hope conceded. 'But you can't blame a man for trying to avoid trouble and annoyance.'

'When you're dealing with the police, by trying to avoid trouble you make it. Who was the man ?'

'It's no use, Inspector. I won't abuse the confidence of a client, even for the police.'

Martineau got to his feet.

'All right,' he said. 'We'll leave it at that—for the time being.'

He left the room by the way he had entered. He went downstairs and out by the front door, where Devery was still waiting.

'He slipped us,' he told the sergeant, 'and Hope won't give me his name. Nevertheless, we may have made a bit of progress.'

He told Devery about his interview with Hope. 'These stockbrokers must be a bit like bankers,' the sergeant said. 'Professional ethics, and all that.'

Martineau snorted. 'Professional hell ! Hope doesn't want to offend a valuable customer.'

He looked at his watch. 'I could do with a pint,' he

said. 'Come on, I'll buy you the odd one in Ella's bar. Then we'll go and see what the canteen has to offer us in the way of lunch.'

They walked in the direction of the Northland Hotel. At a distance, Bert Preston followed them. Now, nobody followed Bert Preston.

6

DURING FRIDAY AFTERNOON, Martineau and Devery interviewed G. Llewellyn Thomas, Reuben George Walters, and Hubert Warren. None of these gentlemen could tell them anything about Inspector McQuade's movements or intentions on Monday evening, though Walters had seen him in his office in the afternoon, and had given him a statement.

'Five down and three to go,' said Martineau as they left Warren's office. 'Drax and Taylor are out of reach until Monday. That leaves Sylvia Paris. I wonder if she's at home now.'

Since Headquarters was almost directly on their way to the inner residential district where Mrs. Paris lived, they returned to Martineau's office. The chief inspector phoned from there, and received an answer.

'Hello,' a woman said, and her voice was vaguely familiar.

'Mrs. Paris ?' Martineau asked, reflecting that outside of an office women seldom answered the telephone in the proper manner.

'Speaking,' the woman said.

'This is Chief Inspector Martineau of the City Police.'

'Hello, Harry ! How are you these days ?'

'I'm fine,' said Martineau, puzzled and playing for time. Sylvia Paris ? Sylvia ? 'Have we met ?' he asked cautiously.

'Now, Harry !' There was merriment in the voice. 'Don't say you've forgotten little Sylvia.'

He knew then. This was a voice from the past. How many years ago ? "Little Sylvia" he remembered as a handsome, strapping blonde girl. At that time she had worked in a city office. He had admired her. There had been an abortive love affair. That had ended when he set eyes on the girl who was now Julia Martineau. But there had been no tears and no regrets. At about that time he had seen Sylvia going into a theatre with her employer. All dressed up like a dog's dinner, he remembered. In such company she had pretended not to see him. That had not hurt him in the least, but probably she thought it had. Since she never knew anything about Julia, no doubt she thought that it was her own conduct which had ended the affair.

'Could that by Sylvia Howard ?' he asked.

'Sylvia Howard as was,' came the merry reply. 'I've been married and widowed since then.'

A widow ! Well, well ! Martineau saw that Devery was watching him curiously. He coughed.

'Aha,' said Sylvia. 'I gather that you are not alone.'

'You're very perceptive. I er—want to see you about a matter connected with the Bassey case.'

'Then come round and see me now, I'm all alone. You'll be just in time for a cocktail. Where are you, the police station ? I'll send my car round for you. I'm dying to see what you look like after all these years.'

Martineau was also curious to see what Mrs. Paris looked like, but he did not say so. It seemed that she had got on in the world, in a material way at least. A car and a chauffeur, look you.

'I'm on my way,' he said.

'The car will be there in five minutes,' she promised.

Martineau put down the phone. He looked at Devery, and thought of the police custom of sending two officers to interview a woman who was alone. That was for the purpose of protecting the officers, from allegations, from temptations, from malicious gossip. He did not know what Mrs. Paris might do or say when he met her. Devery might get a quiet laugh at his expense.

'It turns out that Mrs. Paris is a very old friend of mine,' he said. 'I knew her before she was married.'

'So I assumed, sir.' Devery's manner was just a shade too solemn.

'So I'll go alone to see her. I might get more out of her that way.'

'Oh, undoubtedly, sir.'

'Well, it isn't as if she were a stranger, is it ?'

'Of course it isn't, sir.'

'So you can be getting on with some paper work.'

'Very good, sir.' Devery turned and left the room. Martineau reached for his hat, and thought that the sergeant was too clever by half, sniggering young devil.

He went outside, and waited at the kerb. The sunshine of early evening was pleasant. He scanned the shadowed side of the street, looking for Bert Preston. He could see nothing of the man. He lit a cigarette.

In a few minutes a handsome Bentley car swept quietly to the kerb. The chauffeur alighted. He was small, spare, and elderly, but he was smart and erect in his livery. He touched his cap. 'Inspector Martineau ?' he asked.

'None other,' said the policeman, whose only experience with chauffeurs had been to harry them for parking too long, when he was a constable in uniform.

The chauffeur held open the door of the car. Martineau stepped in. Immediately he turned and looked out through the rear window. He saw Bert Preston at the corner, looking round in dismay for a taxi. There was no taxi, and Preston was too far away to be able to read the number of the car.

The chauffeur appeared to drive steadily, but he had a good car and its speed was deceptive. In six or seven minutes Martineau was alighting in Rothmere Gardens, where a number of big town houses had been converted into luxury flats.

'Perhaps you had better wait. I won't be long,' he said.

'Certainly, sir. I'll wait,' said the chauffeur.

According to the name-plates beside the door, Mrs. Paris had a second-floor flat. Martineau pressed her bell button, and went up the stairs. She was waiting at her door for him. Her hand was outstretched in a hostess gesture of perfect friendliness. 'How nice to see you again, Harry,' she said. 'Do come in.'

He entered the little hallway of the flat. She took his hat and put it in a hall closet. "Not a hair out of place," he thought, as he covertly looked around him. It was a luxury flat all right. The hallway was done out in white and gold.

She took him into her living-room. It was large and sunny, with big windows, and expensively furnished with an eye to ease rather than elegance. There was a settee as big as a bed, and the carpet was rich. The glitter of cut-glass on a side table made the visitor aware that drinks were available. Though large, it was a cosy room with a warm atmosphere. The chairs looked very comfortable.

Having glanced swiftly around, and having observed that five or six brand-new five-pound notes were spread in a careless fan shape on the mantelpiece, Martineau turned to take a good look at his one-time girl friend. He knew that she must be at least thirty-five years old, but she looked younger. Superficially she had changed. The robust girl had been fined down and polished. Now she was a very shapely, beautiful and elegant woman. Her fair skin was fine and clear, and her hair was still the authentic blonde colour without the least touch of red in it. Her dress was very smart, and designed to betray rather than hide the shape of her.

'Well,' he said honestly. 'Time has been very good to you, at any rate.'

She smiled. 'You haven't done so bad yourself, Harry. You're successful. And you're big and strong and handsome.'

'Steady,' he said. 'I'm not handsome.'

'Oh, but you are. I always thought so. But do sit down and I'll get you a drink. I have no maid ; only two day women.'

He took the chair she indicated. She stood smiling down at him. 'What will you have ?' she asked.

He would have liked a pint of draught beer, but he doubted if Mrs. Paris would have such a plebeian brew upon her premises. 'A drop of whisky, if that's all right,' he said.

'But certainly. And I'll have a Martini.' She moved to the side table.

Sitting there, he reflected that she had changed in more than appearance. She had an ease of manner which was very nearly the real thing : very nearly the manner of a woman born and reared in a cultured home and an expensive school. From it he inferred that for quite a number of years she had mixed with people who were, or had enough money to think themselves, of a better class. Real culture she might not have, but she had the gloss of it. There's a million of 'em, he thought. Nevertheless, she was a damned attractive woman.

She brought him his drink, which she put upon a small table beside his chair. With her own drink she moved to the chair opposite. Facing the sunny outdoors, her eyes were brilliantly blue. She crossed her legs, revealing that her calves and ankles were without fault. She drew his attention to this by pulling down her skirt.

'My goodness,' she said. 'It's ages since I had a man in the house. You look just right, Harry. A fair man and a square man, filling that chair as it ought to be filled.'

He smiled in some embarrassment, raised his eyes and said, 'Cheers.' Some women actually were like that, he mused. They would shamelessly slap on the flattery until they got a man believing that they were sincere.

"Break it up," he thought, and aloud he said, 'From that remark I take it that Inspector McQuade wasn't here.'

The clearly defined lines of her eyebrows rose. 'Inspector McQuade ? You mean the man who was murdered ?'

'Yes. He was on the Bassey case. I'm trying to find out where he was on Monday evening. You are one of the people with whom he had not recorded an interview.'

She was smiling again. 'I see,' she said. 'You were wondering if he was here on Monday. No, he was not. I never saw him, and I know precious little about Bassey. He did some business for me, but not much.'

'You do play the stock market, then ?'

She laughed. 'Not really. I know practically nothing about it. But sometimes I get a bit of good information, and I act on it.'

Suddenly, as she concluded that remark, a dark thought crossed her mind. Momentarily her face clouded, and she bit her lip. Then she was smiling again.

He had not failed to notice. 'The tips are not always good ones, eh ?' he queried.

'Not always,' she said, still smiling.

'Well,' he said, looking at his glass, 'I guess that just about closes the interview.'

'The official part. There's no need for you to rush away, is there ? After all, it's been years and years since we met. You did like me once, didn't you ?'

He nodded. She was trying to force him to say that he still liked her, and he was not so sure that he did. All the same, he was aware of her attraction. She was seductive and, he thought, unscrupulous. If she wanted something from a man, she would be a hard woman to resist. Well, there was nothing that an apparently wealthy and carefree woman like her could want from a chief inspector of police. At this moment, he thought, she was merely amusing herself : practising her art.

'Strange how we lost sight of each other altogether,' he said.

'Granchester is a big town,' she replied. 'I moved into a different circle. I was lucky, very lucky. I married a good man who also happened to be rich. We lived in London for about nine years, then he was made chairman of the company and we came back to Granchester. He died, and left everything to me. I had been a good wife to him. I only disappointed him in one thing.'

He nodded again. He liked her better after that little speech. 'The disappointment was—no children ?' he hazarded.

'Correct. He wanted a son. Poor Jim. A better husband a woman couldn't wish to have.'

'How long have you been a widow ?'

'A little over five years.'

'Not from necessity, I'll be bound.'

She smiled. 'No. There have been—offers. I suppose you're married ?'

'Yes. We have one little girl, three years old. We were rather late starting to raise a family.'

'Not great breeders, the Martineaus and the Howards apparently. I wonder what children there would have been if you had married me. I might not have been childless.'

Here we go on another tack, he thought. In those circumstances the seemingly innocent remark could have been calculated to bring an improper picture to a man's mind. The interview was *not* at an end. This woman's talk was leading up to something.

'You don't answer,' she said. 'You're not bearing a grudge over what happened long ago, are you ?'

63

'Not at all. What gives you that impression ?'

'Well, you're sort of reserved. Not once have you called me Sylvia. We're not strangers, you know.'

'You've hit the nail on the head, Sylvia. We *are* strangers. You were a girl of my own class when I knew you. Now you're a sophisticated woman. An extremely sophisticated woman, I imagine.'

'So what ? I've grown up, that's all. We've both grown up. Can you tell me any type in the world which is more sophisticated than a detective inspector ? You should be at ease in *any* society. You're not a bobby on a beat, you're a successful professional man.'

'Today's bobby is tomorrow's inspector. The difference is a matter of service, experience, application and luck.'

'And intelligence and aptitude and courage. You're mature and poised. You're sophisticated, in fact.'

'And being sophisticated, I don't kid very easily.'

'I'd be a fool to try and kid a detective inspector, wouldn't I ? A silly little woman like I am ?'

'You wouldn't be the first woman to try. And wiser men than police inspectors have been kidded.'

'No, I don't grant you that. Lured and tempted and seduced, perhaps, but not kidded. And when I say seduced, I mean it in its true, broad sense.'

'Naturally,' said Martineau, with a polite inclination of the head. 'I wouldn't expect a woman of your standing to mention the word in any other sense.'

And here we go, he mused, talking about seduction—in its broadest sense—before we've been alone for ten minutes. She's clever. And she's after something.

He finished his drink. She rose quickly and took his glass, and went to the side table with it. 'No,' he said, rising also. 'Not another, thank you. I have work to do.'

'You must not go yet,' she said, returning with the drink. 'I—I want to talk to you. Do sit down for just a minute.'

He sat down. He took the drink, but put it on the table near his chair. He waited.

She remained on her feet, standing quite near to him. She held out her hands in a gesture of supplication. Her attitude, almost, was one of surrender. He could have reached up and taken those hands, and pulled her down to him.

'You don't know what it is to be a woman and to have no man to stand up for you,' she said. 'I need help. I've needed it for a year. It wasn't until I saw you today that I realized who could help me. You can, if you will.'

He was cautious. 'As a policeman, you mean ?'

'As a policeman, but unofficially. You can find things out. That's what I want.'

'And what is it I can find out for you ?'

'Well, I lost a lot of money in a stock market deal. I *think* I was swindled. You can find out if I actually *was* swindled. Then you can make the man give me back my shares at the price I sold them.'

'Steady,' he said. 'That's a large order. If I dig up any real evidence about a swindle there's only one thing I can do, and that is to see that the Director of Public Prosecutions gets to know about it. The question of restitution is out of my hands altogether.'

'It need not be. There's no need for a prosecution. You could give the evidence to me.'

He looked at her curiously. 'So that you could put the bite on somebody ?'

'So that I could get back what is rightfully mine.'

'Do you know this man who might have swindled you

'Yes. Have you ever heard of a man called Lionel Hart ?'

'Yes,' said Martineau. 'I have.'

'And do you remember the big fire at Granchester Textiles about a year ago ?'

'Certainly I do.'

'Well, at that time I owned a very big block of G.T.

65

shares, left to me by my husband. They were my biggest single financial asset.'

He nodded. 'Very good shares, I believe. Knowing nothing about shares.'

'They are good shares,' she said warmly. She was not acting now, at any rate, he thought. She was just a woman with a grievance.

'I sold those shares the morning after the fire,' she said. 'Every single one of them. I was misled by lying information. Lionel Hart phoned me first thing in the morning. He said he was getting rid of all his G.T. shares. He told me about the fire, and he said G.T. had temporarily been storing some highly inflammable synthetic yarn—I can't remember the name of it—in a warehouse which wasn't insured for inflammable stuff. He said that the insurance people had found out about it, and weren't going to pay up. It was all a big lie, but I believed it. I sold my shares straight away. It was a million-pound fire and I knew that even a firm as big as G.T. was bound to feel such a loss.'

'Didn't your stockbroker advise you against such a hasty action ?'

'The broker was John Bassey,' she said grimly. 'He took the commission and said nothing.'

'And you didn't consult anyone else ?'

'No,' she admitted. 'I was very friendly with Lionel Hart at that time. And his advice had always been good.'

He thought : Friendly ? With that old turkey gobbler ? Well, let's keep the party clean. Friendly means friendly.

'Lionel had sold his own shares,' she went on, 'and when mine came tumbling after them there was a little panic. They dropped, but not for long. Just long enough for somebody to buy up every available share like lightning, while other people were wondering what to do. Those shares are hard to come by, but somebody got a whole lot of them cheap.'

'And you think that person was Lionel Hart ?'

'I do. He's never been near me since that day. I spoke
to him on the phone, and he was full of apologies. He
said he'd been fooled himself, and he was terribly sorry
because he had led me into it also. I didn't suspect him
then. It was later, when I heard the rumours.'

'What rumours ?'

'Rumours that the fire had been started on purpose by
somebody.'

'The rumours were baseless.'

'I don't think they were. The actual cause of the fire
was never discovered.'

Martineau looked up at her and shook his head. He
was not aware that Superintendent Clay had heard the
same allegation from Leon Crow, and this woman had not
given the hints about Dixie Costello and candle money
which Crow had given to the superintendent. Sylvia's
information and Crow's might have added up to at least
a suspicion, but Clay had not seen fit to say anything to
Martineau about alleged arson.

'The fire experts could find no evidence of foul play,
so how can anyone else find it twelve months later ?' he
wanted to know. 'There'll be no documentary evidence,
you can be sure of that. The only possible evidence would
be in the form of statements and verbal admissions, and
unless a few people were prepared to swear that they saw
somebody start the fire, there wouldn't be enough evidence
for a conviction.'

'But I tell you I don't want a conviction,' she cried.
'I want my shares back. They've made a great difference
to me. Without those dividends I can't live without nibbling
at my capital.'

'Well,' he said. 'You may have been swindled, but if
you were, then somebody had a bright idea as soon as he
heard about the fire. I don't think there was a case of arson.
And, as I have pointed out to you, if there is we can't
prove it.'

'But you can prove a swindle ?'

He thought about that. 'It should be possible to find out whether or not Hart bought your shares. That would be a start.'

'Then, maybe, you could frighten him into letting me have them back,' the woman said hopefully.

'Not me. I'm too busy, anyway. I could report the matter, and some other man would be put on the job. He'd go after Hart, and find out if it was possible to build up a case.'

Mrs. Paris did not give up. She looked, or tried to look, like a little girl who is determined to wear her party dress no matter what the opposition. 'I know you'll help me,' she said. 'I can wait. You'll help me when you've solved this murder. You won't be so busy then.'

He was patient. 'I'm not the man for the job,' he said. 'I can do you the favour of not reporting it at Headquarters, that's all. If I knew of a really good private detective in this town I would recommend him to you, but I don't know one good enough to get the evidence you need. A boss mobster like Dixie Costello might be able to help you, but he would probably rob you at the same time. A good man to keep away from, Mr. Costello.'

She went and leaned on the mantelpiece. 'You'll help me, I know you will,' she said. 'You'll think of something or somebody.'

He rose, leaving his drink still untouched. 'Don't rely on it,' he said drily. She looked hurt by his tone, so he said, 'Sorry I can't do better. And now I'm afraid I must go.'

'I'll get your hat,' she said.

He waited, looking round the room, while she got his hat. She put it into his hands and looked up into his face. 'Don't let me down, Harry,' she said softly.

He smiled at her. 'There's one thing about you,' he said. 'You don't give up, do you ?'

She returned his smile, and he left her. He went down the stairs with a feeling that all was not well. He supposed that he must have left something unsaid, or said something that he should not have said. What could it have been? He was still thinking about it when he stepped out into the street. The sun was well down now, hidden behind houses, but the air seemed still to be full of hazy April sunshine. The chauffeur was still waiting. He opened the door of the Bentley and Martineau stepped in. He put his hat down on the seat beside him. Still pondering, he lit a cigarette.

Then suddenly he knew. The fivers! He had looked around while Sylvia was getting his hat, and they had not been on the mantelpiece. Could Sylvia have planted them on him? He did not think so. She had not even touched him or brushed against him. She could allege that he stole them while she was getting his hat. Ah, the hat! Going for it, she had been just a little longer than she ought to have been.

The car was in motion. He looked at the chauffeur. The little man appeared to be looking straight ahead. If this was another conspiracy, it was extremely doubtful that he would be in it. Nevertheless, when Martineau moved the hat he kept it well below the man's line of vision in the driving mirror. Holding the hat upside down, he turned back part of the leather sweat band with his finger and saw a five-pound note. It had been folded lengthwise so that it could be hidden by the sweat band. Overlapping it there was another note. He turned back the sweat band all round and found six of the notes, neatly arranged around the hat. Nimble fingers had put them there. It had been a neat job quickly done.

Martineau put the notes together, folded them, and stuffed them down behind the seat cushion of the car. He put his hat on his head. He pondered. Could there be anything else? Unobtrusively, but thoroughly, he went through his pockets. He found nothing there which was not his own property.

For the rest of the short journey he thought about Sylvia Paris, with feelings of curiosity rather than anger. Could Sylvia be the person whom Devery had called Bashful ? No, he decided. But she might lead him to Bashful. She might very well do that.

When he had alighted from Sylvia Paris's car at the police station, Martineau went into the C.I.D. office. Devery was still there, standing at the long, high desk and typing like an expert. He looked up expectantly, with a faint grin.

'Any luck, sir ?' he asked.

'All the luck in the world,' said Martineau, also grinning, and in a way which surprised and baffled the sergeant. 'But no information about McQuade.'

His grin widened when he saw how Devery was looking at him. 'Oh yes, I've had a drink,' he said. 'And now I can go and have a quiet evening at home for a change.'

'Good,' said Devery. He removed his report from the typewriter. He put on the cover.

Smiling wickedly, Martineau watched the operation. 'Oh, no,' he said. '*You're* not going home. You can stay and think your naughty thoughts here. In a little while there will be a job for you.'

'What sort of a job ?'

'Mrs. Sylvia Paris will be on the phone. She'll go high. She might even go to the Chief. But whoever she makes her complaint to, it will eventually get to Chief Superintendent Clay. I'm going to see him and advise him to put the matter in your hands. Now, here's the drill. Mrs. Paris will be oh, so distressed. She'll hardly like to say it, but there *were* half-a-dozen fivers on the mantelpiece when Mr. Martineau arrived, and they weren't there after he had gone. Oh yes, she did leave him alone with the money while she went to get his hat. She'll know that police inspectors aren't overpaid, but really ! Stealing ! She'll scarcely be able to believe it, but there it will be.'

Devery was staring, utterly astounded for once in his life. Martineau went on, enjoying himself somewhat : 'She'll happen to know the numbers of the notes because she got them from the bank this morning, and they run in sequence. You'll go to see her and'—he looked around, and saw a plain clothes man at the other end of the room— 'you'll take Cassidy with you. You, too, will have difficulty in believing that a police inspector would take her money, and you'll suggest that she might have mislaid it. You'll ask permission to search the flat, and she won't very well be able to refuse you. You'll search, and anything interesting you'll take note of. Then you'll search her car, in her presence or the chauffeur's. It's a Bentley, sage green ; I'll give you the number in a minute. In the back of the car, stuffed behind the seat, you'll find the money. If it isn't there, you can go to work on the chauffeur, because he will have found it and pinched it. When you've returned the money to Mrs. Paris you'll make out your report and then you can go home. Is all clear ?'

'Perfectly clear, sir. Where was it planted ?'

'Inside the sweat band of my hat. I was damn lucky to find it.'

'I'll say you were. Coo, that was deadly. With Mrs. Paris demanding a prosecution, neither the Chief nor any-one else would have been able to get you out of that one. She ought to be shot.'

'I'm going to see the boss and arrange to have her watched. She might lead us to Bashful.'

'I say. If she hadn't let you see the money in the first place, you never would have found it.'

'That is so. Letting me see the money was one of the inexplicable errors these people make. Unless she did it because she thought it might strengthen her case somehow. Anyway, she's your pigeon. I'm going to see the Super and then I'm off home. I'd better not be around when the fun starts.'

71

7

AT TEN O'CLOCK that night, Martineau received a telephone call at his home. The caller was Devery. The sergeant wanted to know how long he was supposed to wait for Mrs. Paris to make her complaint.

'Hasn't she made a move yet?' asked Martineau in surprise. 'Well, that's odd.'

'It occurs to me that she's been trying to contact some of the top brass, and failed to do so.'

'Could be. Now I suppose she'll leave it till morning. You'd better go home to bed. I'm sorry you had a wasted evening.'

'That's all right, sir,' Devery replied cheerfully, because he always held firmly to the opinion that grumbling about matters of that sort in C.I.D. work sometimes was harmful and never was any good for the man who grumbled. He rang off. The evening had been wasted, and that was that.

Martineau returned to his armchair and meditated briefly about Mrs. Paris. By delaying her complaint she was definitely weakening her case. Or so it seemed. And, though she did not know it, she had no case. He dismissed her from his mind, and returned his attention to the matter which had been occupying it, namely the Boston Symphony Orchestra playing the *Symphonie Fantastique* of Berlioz, a piece of music of which both he and his wife Julia were very fond.

That was Friday. Saturday was sunny and warm from

the start, lovely weather which is always appreciated in England because there is seldom enough of it. Martineau hummed a tune while he shaved. Work or no work, he always liked a fine Saturday morning. He went off to work in good time, and walked into the C.I.D. at exactly nine o'clock. Devery was already there.

'Morning, sir,' the sergeant said. 'Did you see Bert Preston as you came in ?'

'I never gave him a thought,' Martineau replied. 'Did you see him ?'

'No. What's the betting he won't be with us any more ? I'm of the opinion that Bashful already knows we spotted Bert.'

'You could be right. Anyway, we're not worried, are we ? The person we have to worry about is Mrs. Paris. What's her game ? Why hasn't she weighed in with a complaint yet ?'

'I don't know. There's your phone, sir.'

The telephone in Martineau's office was ringing. He went to take the call, and Devery followed. 'A person calling himself Number Twelve wishes to speak to you, sir,' the communications clerk said.

'Put him on,' said Martineau, and a moment later he was listening to the voice of Bert Preston.

'Not a word have I heard, and no more money,' said Preston. 'I don't like working for nowt. What shall I do ?'

'I think you can consider yourself dishonourably discharged, Bert,' said Martineau. 'You can go home and read the Racing Special. But if you do hear anything, don't forget to let me know.'

'Right you are,' said Preston, relieved. He rang off.

'That's the last of him,' said Martineau, and then the phone rang again. The police operator said, 'A Mrs. Paris wishes to speak to you, sir.'

'Put her on,' he said. And to Devery, 'Here we go.'

'Hello there, good morning,' said Mrs. Paris, in the

merry way which seemed to be her telephone manner. 'How is my handsome inspector this morning ?'

'I'm very well,' said Martineau. 'And you ?'

'I *could* be very cross. You're a naughty man, and a very clever one. My chauffeur has just brought me six five-pound notes which he found in the car.'

'How nice for you,' said the policeman.

'It isn't nice at all. I intended to phone you this morning and tell you to look for it in your hat. It was a surreptitious gift. A little present as a reward for the help you're going to give me.'

'I don't accept presents,' said Martineau cruelly, 'and I'm not going to give you any help. Good morning.' He put down the receiver.

Devery opened his mouth to make some comment, but he was deterred by the look on his superior's face. Martineau was scowling. He had dealt a rebuff, to a woman, which had been like a slap in the face. And, to a woman, that was something which he did not like to do.

'That's the end of that,' he growled. 'And I'm getting weary of listening to liars. We'll get on with the job and we'll talk to somebody truthful for a change. We haven't yet been to see young Tess McQuade.'

'Ah yes, little Tess,' said Devery, and then suddenly he slapped the fist of one hand into the palm of the other. 'My word, I never thought,' he said, and then he came out with an item of gossip which made Martineau stare.

'Say that again,' the chief inspector commanded.

Devery said it again, and went on : 'Cassidy wouldn't pass it on to me if it wasn't true, would he ? He's about the most truthful Irishman I ever met.'

'Cassidy is all right,' Martineau concurred. 'And you say he saw this with his own eyes ?'

'I think you'd better ask him, sir.'

'I will,' said Martineau. 'What turn is he ?'

'Evening Duty, sir.'

'So we'll find him at home. Spicecake Lane, isn't it ?'

'Yes sir,' said Devery.

Martineau rang for a car, and the two men were driven two miles to Spicecake Lane, where a number of neat little houses had been built by the police authority. Detective Constable Cassidy lived with his English wife in one of the houses.

Mrs. Cassidy answered the door. She admitted Martineau and Devery, having a smile and a pleasant word for them both. Then she returned to the kitchen, where she had been busy when their knock came on the door.

Cassidy had been on duty until 2 a.m. or later. Now he was newly arisen. He had had some breakfast and he was reading the morning paper. He was dismayed by the sight of his colleagues, and the dismay was palpable. When a detective officer is visited at his home by a chief inspector and a sergeant, it is usually a sign of trouble for the D.O. And not unimportant trouble, either.

'Sit down, sir. Sit down, Sergeant,' he said, bustling about and offering chairs, vainly trying to hide his uneasiness. 'Would you like a cup of coffee, now ?'

'No, thanks,' said Martineau, sitting down.

'Well, could I be offering you a cigarette ?'

'No, thanks,' said the inspector, and then as tragedy deepened in Cassidy's eyes he said, 'Here, have one of mine.'

Cassidy, a man six feet tall and as broad as a door, took the cigarette gratefully. 'And what could I do for you, sir ?' he asked, more cheerful now.

'It's a bit of gossip about young Theresa McQuade,' was the crisp answer.

Instantly Cassidy was uneasy again, and he gave Devery a reproachful look. 'Sure I wouldn't be putting about talk against the daughter of a superior officer,' he protested. 'But it was so unnatural-like I just mentioned it to the sergeant here.'

'Did you mention it to anyone else?'

'Yes, sir,' said Cassidy honestly. 'I mentioned it to Detective Officer Ducklin.'

'Is that all?'

'That is all, sir.'

'H'm. Now mention it to me. Tell me all about it.'

'There's not much to tell. Tess McQuade was talking to Barry Hill, that's all. I watched 'em.'

'You *watched* them?'

'I did, sir. Me wife was with me at the time. It was in Essex Street, and they were on the other side. Tess and Hill, I mean. I said to the missus, "We'd better hang on for a second. Somebody is going to be yelling for a policeman any minute now".'

'I see. Your first thought was that Hill had accosted Tess.'

'What else could I think, sir? That boy and Mick McQuade's daughter! If she had let out one yip I'd a-been across there banging his head on the concrete.'

Martineau smiled, because Cassidy was quite capable of doing that very thing. 'So you watched?'

'We stood at the kerb for three or four minutes, Mrs. Cassidy and me. She'll bear me out, only of course she didn't know Barry Hill from Oliver Cromwell. But Tess never saw us, nor neither did Hill. If ever I saw a girl trying to put the 'fluence on a fellow it was Tess. And he was the same. They were like a courting couple, and that's a fact. You ask my wife.'

'No, I'll take your word for it, Cassidy,' said Martineau. He sat in thought. Here was something. Barry Hill was a mobster, a razor boy. He was one of the younger, brighter and smarter of Dixie Costello's men. As one of Dixie's followers, his activities were at the worst criminal and at the best shady. At Dixie's bidding he would help to intimidate, and extort money from, bookmakers at flapping tracks and racecourses. He would be concerned with doping horses and greyhounds, running ringers, working the pencil game, "fixing" prize-fights and wrestling matches, slicing, maiming, and laming the enemies of Dixie, and putting into profitable operation any other of the unlawful or immoral schemes which Dixie's sharp brain evolved. He was a crook : a skilled, wily, incorrigible crook at twenty-five years of age. And, thought Martineau, he was dancing round the maypole with the daughter of Detective Inspector Robert McQuade.

'Does young Tess understand exactly what Barry Hill does for a living ?' he wondered aloud.

'I wouldn't know that, sir,' said Cassidy. 'All I know is what I told you.'

Martineau nodded, and again there was silence in the room. The inspector meditated upon the matter of theories. There was one theory, and a feasible one, that McQuade had been murdered because he had stumbled across the path of some man whom he recognized as a criminal, and to whom he constituted a danger. Now there was another theory, and while it was not yet the better one, it was the one more to Martineau's liking.

His eyes narrowed and his nostrils distended slightly when he thought of it. It was work more to his taste than the business of quizzing accountants and stockbrokers and their clients. It was as if a wolfhound, while sniffing at the tracks of a hare, had suddenly come upon the trail of the savage beast who was his natural enemy. From now on, for a little while at least, Martineau would be hunting in familiar country, and his quarry would be the sort of creature who had kept him busy for twenty years.

'When did this meeting occur ?' he asked. 'How long ago ?'

Cassidy pondered. 'Let's see, it was on a Saturday afternoon, two or three weeks back.' He called out. 'Eve ! Have you a minute ?'

Mrs. Cassidy appeared in the kitchen doorway. If she

was full of curiosity anent Martineau's visit, she concealed it very well.

'Was it two or three weeks last Saturday when we saw Tess McQuade talking to that fellow ?' her husband asked.

'Three weeks last Saturday,' she answered without hesitation. And to prevent further query, 'You were on week-end leave.'

'Ah, so I was,' said Cassidy. 'Three weeks last Saturday was the day, sir.'

'Thank you,' said Martineau. He smiled at Mrs. Cassidy, and she went back to the kitchen.

He considered the implications of the Tess McQuade-Barry Hill affair. It had certainly been in existence three weeks and two days before the murder of Inspector McQuade, and possibly it had been in existence for some time longer than that. But three weeks was enough. In three weeks there could assuredly have been developments resulting in a murderous quarrel. Three weeks was a long time to a girl of nineteen and a man of twenty-five who were infatuated with each other. Or even if it were only a case of infatuation on one side and hot lust on the other.

'What do we know about Barry Hill ?' he asked. He knew a good deal himself, but he hoped for information from these younger men.

'He's a hard boy,' said Devery. 'Juvenile delinquent. Borstal. But I don't know anything after that. I think he's technically clean since Borstal.'

'Since he took up with Costello, you mean ?'

'That's right, sir. Costello's boys don't get into trouble. Not when they're obeying orders, at any rate. But I've heard tales about Hill.'

'So have I,' said Cassidy.

'What sort of tales ?'

'He's violent, even for that crowd,' said Devery. 'Always ready to do somebody, especially if he has a knuckleduster handy.'

'He's just a dressed-up cut-throat,' said Cassidy. 'A nice crease to his trousers, a shine to his shoes, clean fingernails, fancy handkerchief in one pocket, razor in the other, and lay your face open as soon as look at you.'

'Razor. Knuckleduster. What else ?'

Cassidy looked puzzled, but Devery said, 'Do you mean a gun, sir ?'

'Yes,' said Martineau. 'Have you ever heard of Barry Hill carrying a gun ?'

'I haven't,' said Devery, and Cassidy shook his head. But Cassidy was no longer bewildered. Now he knew what was in Martineau's mind. He felt very good and important about that. He had been the means of uncovering a murder suspect.

'Some men like guns for their own sake,' said Martineau. 'They can't bring themselves to throw them away. The murder gun hasn't been found yet. The murderer might still have it.'

There was a brief silence, and Martineau went on, '*If* Mick McQuade knew that his daughter was fooling around with a crook, that is a fact which we must establish. With that, we can see a motive for his murder.'

'In hot blood,' said Devery. 'In the heat of a quarrel.'

'Possibly. I happen to know that McQuade was a brave man. Also, his blood was as Irish as yours, Cassidy. Also, he worshipped his daughter, especially since he lost his wife. All that might lead us to think that he would go for Hill like a bull at a gate, and yet I'm doubtful.'

'He was a canny man, sir,' said Cassidy.

'He was. If it had been a matter of stopping an affair between Barry Hill and my daughter, or your daughter, we know how he would have handled it. It is the fact that it was his own daughter which leaves us in doubt. How do you imagine he would feel, Cassidy ?'

'He would be pierced to the heart, sir.'

'I'm sure he would. So we don't know what he would

do. But we must remember one thing ; he was a man who liked to use his brains in all circumstances where the use of brains were possible.'

Devery interposed. 'What about the Gutteridge touch, sir ? Do you think Hill is the sort who would shoot a dead man's eyes out ?'

'You know the belief about a murdered man's eyes. Hill might think there is something in it. He may be a smart Alec, but he's still an ignorant hooligan. But in any case we're not going to be misled by the assumption that any certain person is or is not the type of man who would do this or that. Nobody knows what anybody will do under pressure.'

So then it was only a question of ways and means, because there was no doubt about what to do. Get hold of Hill. Get him quickly, and quietly if possible. Get him safely inside for interrogation and then, then only, send out men to make inquiries about him. To handle the matter in any other way would probably result in Hill learning that the police were curious about him. Then, if he were the murderer, he would have time to get rid of his gun, prepare an alibi, anything. Get Hill first, that was the thing.

Cassidy was looking anxious again. He was not due to go on duty until six o'clock in the evening. He wanted to be in this thing. He knew nothing about any alternative theory. Since Hill was a crook, and was under suspicion, and had a motive, then he thought that Hill must be the man who had killed Mick McQuade. To have a hand in his arrest would be the chance of a lifetime.

'Are you going to pull him in, sir ?' he asked hopefully. 'I'm ready. Three pairs of hands are better than two when you're tackling a man who might have a gun. I can be with you in a jiffy.'

'All right,' said Martineau. 'Get your shoes on.'

While Martineau waited, he visualized the man they

would be seeking. A tallish, elegantly built, elegantly dressed young man. A handsome young man with white teeth and bright brown eyes and smooth black hair. A spirited, wisecracking young man whom the girls would readily fancy. A young man who would "lay your face open as soon as look at you."

8

THE DECISION to take in Barry Hill was one thing ; the finding of him was quite another. Martineau dared not "put out the word" for him. The situation was too touchy and uncertain for that. The man had to be found before anyone except Martineau and his helpers knew that he was being sought.

Hill had parents in Granchester ; he was Granchester born and bred. But he did not live with his parents. He had parted in anger from his father, a coal merchant in a small way of business, soon after he had ended his last period of "training and correction" in a Borstal Institution. Now, his last known address was in the Rubber Lane area, which was a district of theatrical lodging houses, furnished rooms, boarding houses, and—until the police found them and raided them—brothels and gaming houses.

But Martineau did not seek Hill at his lodgings. That was the last place to go. The time, the middle of the forenoon, was right for finding the man in one of the clubs, cafés, or billiards rooms which were the haunts of the Dixie Costello mob. Using Cassidy and Devery as scouts because, though fairly well-known as detectives, they were not so well-known as himself, he searched the likely places in the centre of the city. The half-past eleven opening time came, and he turned his attention to the pubs. Costello himself was found having a drink-before-lunch at the Northland Hotel, in company with a gorgeously over-dressed young woman known as Popsie, who was his current paramour. Others of the gang, Ned Higgs, Herman Waddy, Peter Riskin, Bert Sloan, Sammy Orpington, Wally Waters, and a man of terrifying appearance and reputation known as The Dog—his name was Wolfe—were likewise found in places where they could be expected to be, and engaged as they might be expected to be engaged, namely, consuming intoxicating liquor and studying racing form. Those men lived by, and to some extent for, all forms of gambling.

Cassidy and Devery exchanged no more than a nod or a word or a hostile stare with these individuals. They left them with no clue as to the identity of the person they sought, though it was obvious that they were seeking somebody. That was nothing to worry about. The coppers were always seeking somebody. Very likely they were after some mug who had been pinching lead sheeting, or scrap brass, or some other mugs' commodity. The Costello mob were above such humble forms of larceny.

So, while Martineau succeeded in combing the town without arousing suspicion or alarm among friends of the man he sought, his hunt was, for a time, unsuccessful. He began to consider other possibilities. Hill might be pigging it in bed at his lodgings, he might have gone to any one of three race meetings, he might even—it seemed like sacrilege —be at the home of the late Inspector McQuade, pursuing openly now his courtship of McQuade's daughter.

Martineau was standing in Lacy Street, wondering what to do next, when he saw Hill hurry to a public telephone box not ten yards away. Hill entered the box, inserted the usual four pennies in the pay slot, and quickly dialled a number, obviously a number he knew well. He began to talk to somebody, and then he listened, and then he talked again. Martineau moved nearer to the box, and stood with his back to the wall of a public-house. Hill, half turned away from him and absorbed in conversation, did not see him.

Devery and Cassidy emerged from the pub. 'No luck, sir,' said the sergeant, just a little despondent.

'Never mind,' said Martineau, smiling kindly at him. 'We'll get him in a minute, when he's finished his call.'

Devery looked round in a startled way. He saw the telephone box, and the man inside it. 'Well, blow me down !' he breathed. And aloud he said, 'Shall I call the car up ?'

'Not yet. It will be better if he hangs up before he becomes aware of us. Then he can't pass anything on to the person he's now talking to.'

'I wonder who that is. I don't suppose he'll ever tell us.'

'No, I don't suppose he will,' said Martineau, unconcerned.

They waited. Hill was listening now, and as he did so he looked this way and that at the world outside the glass-walled box. But he did not turn his head round far enough to see the three detectives.

Then the call was ended. Hill cradled the telephone. Martineau said, 'Get him now.'

As Hill stepped out of the box, Devery and Cassidy were there on both sides of him. Each seized an arm and a wrist. Hill tried to pull away, but relaxed when Martineau appeared before him. The inspector stepped to the kerb and waved. His attendant police car came up. Hill was put into the rear of it, between Devery and Cassidy. Martineau took the seat beside the driver. The car moved off towards Headquarters. Not a word had been spoken. The arrest had been quick and quiet, as Martineau had wanted it to be. Scarcely half-a-dozen people on the busy sidewalk had seen it happen.

At Headquarters, Martineau had the suspect taken to the interrogation room. He called a clerk, who took the seat at the small table in the corner. Hill was searched for weapons. He had neither razor, knife, cosh, knuckleduster, nor gun.

He was told to sit at the middle table, and Martineau took the seat opposite. Devery stood behind Hill, and Cassidy stood by the door.

The inspector looked at his prisoner, and received an impassive stare in return. 'Surprised ?' he asked.

'No,' said Hill, in a tone of tough resignation.

'You expected it ?'

'No, but I'm never surprised at what the coppers do. What is it this time ?'

'Murder.'

'Oh, that.'

'Are you still courting Tess McQuade ?'

'Yep. Steady. Any objections ?'

'I'm not in the position to object. But Inspector McQuade was. Did he know about it ?'

'No, he didn't.'

'Are you sure of that ?'

'I'm as sure as I can be. He never said anything to Tess. She would have told me.'

'Did he say anything to *you* ?'

'No. We didn't meet.'

'What were you doing last Monday night, from six o'clock onwards ?'

'I don't have to tell you.'

'No, you don't, if you want me to keep you here.'

'That's different. I don't want you to spoil Saturday for me. I was in a spieler from four o'clock till half-past eight. I can't tell you where, but I can tell you who I was with.'

'Some of the boys, I suppose ?'

'Yes. Waddy, Sloan and Waters. They'll tell you I wasn't mixed up in any murder, but they won't tell you just where I was.'

'What was the game ?'

'Dice.'

'Did you win ?'

'No, I lost a packet. Nearly fifty nicker.'

'Who was the main winner ?'

'A fellow called Reggie Ricks.'

Martineau looked up. 'You heard that, Cassidy ?'

'Yes sir. And I know all the men he's mentioned.'

'Very well. Take someone with you and go and see them. Separately. Let them talk as much as they like, and take it all down in statement form.'

'Yessir.' Cassidy went out.

Martineau said to Hill, 'So you had a ready-made alibi. I rather thought you might have. Waddy, Sloan, Waters and Ricks. What a shower.'

Hill grinned. 'They're witnesses, just the same.'

'What time did you say you left the spieler ?'

'Half-past eight. I went straight to Shirwell from there, and met Tess McQuade at the end of the street where she lives.'

'What time ?'

'Ten minutes to nine. I remember the time because I was five minutes late.'

'How long did you stay with Tess ?'

'Till eleven o'clock. We went in Shirwell Park and sat on a seat.'

'And after you left Tess ?'

'I went straight home to bed.'

Martineau was silent for a while. The doctors and laboratory men had been unanimously of the opinion that Inspector McQuade had been killed between nine o'clock and ten. It was extremely unlikely that all of them could be wrong. Therefore, Tess McQuade was Hill's material witness. He did not need his gaming house alibi. If Hill had faked that alibi—and it smelt to high heaven—he had done so as a precaution because he knew that the police would question him about the murder of his sweetheart's father. Therefore he did not know what time the murder had been committed. Therefore he had not committed it.

That was how it looked. But behind Hill there was a blustering, boisterous man with a very subtle brain. Hill could have taken his troubles to Dixie Costello, and Costello could have arranged that alibi with the intention of leading the police to make the deductions which Martineau had that very moment made.

The inspector turned his thoughts to the real alibi. That had not yet been checked, but he was certain that Hill would not have brought in Tess as a witness unless he had been sure that she would corroborate what he had said. And if Tess corroborated, there were three alternative possibilities. The first, Barry Hill was innocent of the crime. The second, he was guilty and Tess was lying for him, not knowing that she was shielding her father's murderer. The third, he was guilty and Tess was accessory to the murder. That, mused the policeman, was unthinkable but not impossible. Tess might not have loved her father as much as he had loved her. Because she was McQuade's daughter she was not necessarily an angel. In Martineau's mind there was already one black mark against her : she was consorting with a crook. In a manner of speaking, she had gone over to the enemy.

'Does Tess know exactly how you are making a living ?' he asked.

Hill's grin was slightly crooked. The question had touched a raw spot somewhere. 'She has a rough idea,' he replied.

'And does she approve ?'

'No, she does not. She's on the reforming lark. She's given me the ultimatum : I part company with Dixie Costello, or she parts company with me.'

'And what is your answer to that ?'

'I'm leaving Dixie. I'm looking for a job.'

'Does Dixie know ?'

'Not yet.'

'Well, I won't tell him' said Martineau, interested in

spite of his disbelief, based on bitter experience, in the permanent redemption of hardened young crooks of Hill's type. 'What sort of a job are you wanting ?'

'Any sort of a straight job connected with racing or bookmaking. It's the only thing I know anything about.'

Martineau shook his head, not because he disapproved, but because any Granchester bookmaker who employed one of the Costello mob would need to go and see a brain specialist.

'I know what you're thinking,' said Hill. 'But I'll find something.'

'I hope you do,' said the policeman sincerely. 'Do you mind if we search your lodgings, or do I have to get a warrant ?'

'You have my full permission to search. I'm clear of this thing, and I want you to be sure of it. I wouldn't hurt a hair of the head of Tess's father.'

'You seem to be properly smitten.'

'I guess I am,' Hill admitted. 'She's a grand kid.'

'How long has it been going on ?'

'Six or seven weeks, that's all.'

'How did you come to meet Tess ?'

'I've known her all her life, practically. I was brought up in Shirwell, you know. We lived in the same street, where my father lives now. We went to the same school, though I was a lot older than she was. I hadn't seen her for years, and I met her in Howard Street one day. She'd grown up and I didn't recognize her at first. But she recognized me, and she spoke. We stopped to talk and—well, that was it.'

Martineau nodded. He had suddenly remembered something. There was at least one other member of the force who knew about the Tess McQuade-Barry Hill affair. 'Wait here. I'll be back,' he said to Devery. He went out into the main office and looked at the duty sheet. Detective Officer Ducklin was on week-end leave. He said to a plain clothes man : 'Do you happen to know if Ducklin has a telephone ?' and the man replied, 'Yes, sir. He has.'

Martineau went to his own office, and the switchboard operator put him through to Ducklin's home. The man himself answered the call.

'Now, Ducklin,' said Martineau. 'Do you remember Cassidy telling you something about Tess McQuade and Barry Hill ?'

'Yessir,' came the prompt reply.

'Did you mention it to anyone else ? Nobody is going to be annoyed with you if you did, but I must know for certain.'

'I mentioned it to nobody, sir.'

'Not even to Inspector McQuade ?'

'No, sir. No fear !'

'All right. Thank you, Ducklin.' Martineau put down the telephone. He returned to the interrogation room. It did indeed look as if Hill was going to be completely in the clear.

'I'm going to leave you in the outer office,' he said to Hill. 'I shall probably be about an hour. I shall phone through for you to be released as soon as I can.'

'Fair enough, Inspector,' said Hill. 'I think you'll find that everything is as I said it would be.'

'And I'm afraid he's going to be right,' said Martineau in an aside to Devery as they walked through the outer office. 'I think this will be one promising line of enquiry which will bring us to a dead end.'

He saw the duty inspector and arranged for a search crew to be sent to Hill's lodgings, with instructions also for the crew to question the young man's landlady. Then he called for a car to take him and Devery to Shirwell. As they alighted outside the McQuade house they were seen from a window. Tess McQuade opened the front door as they stepped up to it.

'Hello, Mr. Martineau,' she said, and she smiled at Devery. 'Won't you come in ?'

They entered, and in the little living-room Martineau looked around. He had not been in the house for some time, but he could see no change. The furniture gleamed, and the hearth was tidy. Tess was a good little house-keeper.

He took both the girl's hands and looked into her face. She looked rather peaked, and that was to be expected. She was a small girl with a good shape, pretty, but in no way extraordinary ; not at all the sort of girl to steal the heart of a sharp character like Barry Hill. But she had done so. Perhaps, Martineau reflected, like the Rose of Tralee, it was the truth in her eyes which had drawn Hill to her.

'How are you, Tess ?' he asked gently.

Her eyes filled with tears, and it occurred to Martineau that he ought to have visited the daughter of his old friend earlier than this. But he had been busy. She had been seen by detectives. She had given a comprehensive statement to the effect that she had not seen her father after he left the house on Monday morning, and the house itself had been thoroughly searched for any article or document which might help in the investigation of his murder. Only Tess's own movements had not been questioned. Until now.

She freed her hands and dried her eyes. 'Silly of me,' she murmured.

'A little weep does you good sometimes,' said the inspector, banally enough. 'You're a brave girl.'

'Is there any news yet ?' she wanted to know.

Martineau could not be anything but straightforward with Mick McQuade's daughter. He would not get his information by subterfuge. 'No news,' he said. 'Except that I've been talking to that young man of yours.'

Her eyes widened. 'Barry ? What has he got to do with it ?'

'Did your father know about him ?'

'No,' she replied. And then somewhat uncertainly, 'At least I don't think so.'

'You're not sure ?'

'Well, when I was getting ready to go out on Sunday night he asked me if I had a young man, and I said yes, I had.'

'And naturally he asked you who the young man was ?'

'Yes. And I said I didn't want to tell him just yet. He asked me why I wouldn't tell him, and I told a big lie. I said I wasn't sure yet whether or not I really liked this fellow. He just smiled and said I'd better be sure before I brought him home.'

'You know he would eventually have found out ?'

'Oh, yes. I wanted to be the one to tell him, when Barry had settled down in a proper job and sort of proved himself. Last Sunday I just daren't tell him.'

'I see. Did he mention the matter again ?'

'No, not at all,' Tess answered. Tears came again. She dried them away.

'And was his manner quite normal when you came in that night ?'

'Yes.'

'And on Monday morning ?'

'Yes. What did you say to Barry ?'

'Nothing for you to distress yourself about. Did you see him on Monday ?'

'Oh, yes. Monday night.'

'At what time ?'

'Ten to nine. We went in the park. We were there till nearly eleven.'

'Was he with you all the time ?'

'Yes. You don't think he did it, do you ?'

'He couldn't have done it if he was with you.'

'Oh, I see.' She smiled. 'You were just checking up on everything, like you have to do.'

'Something like that. May I use your phone ?'

She said that of course he could use the phone. He called Headquarters, and was put through to the C.I.D. 'Is that Goodwin ?' he said to the clerk who was keeping an eye on Barry Hill. 'Tell that young fellow he can go home now.'

While he made the call, Devery wrote a brief statement in his pocket-book. He read it over to Tess, and she signed it.

'Just for the record, my dear,' said Martineau, as she returned Devery's pen. 'Now bear up, young woman. Keep the old chin up. I'll be calling again, to see how you're going on. I'm going to make sure that young Hill treats you right.'

'Oh, he will, Mr. Martineau. You just don't know how good he is.'

The inspector reflected rather grimly that he had more knowledge of Barry Hill's badness than his goodness, but he made no comment. He and Devery took their leave, and went out to their car.

'Well, that's Barry Hill, that was,' he said as he closed the door of the car. And to the driver he said, 'We'll just round the job off by having a word with Dixie Costello. He's worth turning up any day.'

9

DIXIE COSTELLO lived in the middle of town, in a flat in
All Saints Road, above a small restaurant which he owned.
As the police car approached, its occupants observed that
Mr. Costello was at home. His new ivory-white Rolls-Royce
stood at the kerb near the restaurant, and the woman known
as Popsie was sitting in the seat beside the driver's, apparently waiting for her lord and master to emerge from the
flat.

The door which led to the flat's private stairway was
open. Without a glance at Popsie, Martineau went to the
door and pressed the bell button. Popsie immediately got
out of the car. With cold hauteur which was somewhat
spoiled by a sidelong glance to observe its effects, she
minced past the inspector and the sergeant and disappeared
up the stairs.

'H'm, not a bad leg,' said Devery, with a measure of
approval.

'She's a strumpet,' said Martineau shortly. 'I don't
know how he finds 'em.'

'He doesn't,' Devery rejoined. 'They find him.'

Popsie reappeared at the head of the stairs. 'Will you
come up ?' she called, as distant as Everest. Policemen,
apparently, were on her list of things not mentioned in
polite conversation.

The two detectives went up, and entered the flat. The
big living room was furnished and decorated in a style
which indicated that Dixie had had the help of an expert

with it. Dixie was standing at the mirror over the fireplace, carefully fastening a diamond stickpin in his tie. Popsie had flounced into an armchair, from which she sulkily watched him.

'Come in, come in,' said Dixie, without turning round. 'Make yourselves at home.'

He was a broad but compactly built man of medium height ; a hard, tough, rather handsome man in his early forties. He was dressed impeccably in very good clothes, but the diamonds on fingers, tie and shirt cuffs emphasized rather than concealed the fact that he did not spring from an upper bracket of society. He had fought his way to a position of power in his own villainous world, and he had been ruthless and intelligent enough to hold that position. Nowadays, a number of legitimate enterprises were his official source of income, but the real sources were still gambling and gambling houses, and racecourse and dog-track rackets. When the black market had been a profitable business, he had had his hands in it up to the elbows, and at that time, too, he had been suspected of organizing large-scale robberies of foodstuffs and goods in short supply. Martineau was still prepared to suspect him of anything from murder to mayhem ; anything, that is, except the running of houses of prostitution. Dixie had never been a pimp. In that sense he was clean.

When the diamond was adjusted to his satisfaction, Dixie turned, rubbing his hands. 'It's been a long time since I had a visit from the coppers,' he said hospitably. 'What will you have to drink ?'

'Nothing, thanks,' said Martineau. 'Not just now.'

'Well, well. Then what can I do for you ?'

'I have an inquiry about one of your boys, Barry Hill. He is one of your bevy of flat-nosed beauties, isn't he ?'

'I'll back my lads for looks against a crowd of coppers, any time,' said Dixie with equanimity. 'What's Barry been doing ?'

'Just making me curious.'

'He could sit still and do that, any time. I thought you were supposed to be busy on that murder job.'

'I am.'

For the first time, Dixie showed some uneasiness. 'Look here,' he said. 'Cards on the table. Has Barry been doing something I don't know about ? Was McQuade after him for something ?'

'He may have been, but that's nothing for you to worry about. Hill wasn't operating behind your back, so far as I know.'

Dixie was relieved. 'I'm glad of that,' he said. 'I like Barry, but he's been a lad who's needed watching. I didn't want to have to set The Dog on him. What's the tie-up between Barry and McQuade ?'

Martineau pondered. He had promised not to tell Dixie that Hill was a potential deserter from his gang. He had not promised to be silent about Tess McQuade.

'There's no harm in telling you,' he said deliberately. 'Barry is courting McQuade's daughter.'

There was a small sound from Popsie : surprise and indignation. Martineau turned to look at her.

'Take no notice of her,' said Dixie. 'Barry used to kid her on a bit. He thinks I don't know about it. *She* thinks everything in trousers should be wanting to get into bed with her.'

'Don't drag me into this, you rat,' said Popsie.

'Then be silent, or I'll shut your mouth with the back of my hand.'

Martineau pretended to ignore this domestic interchange. 'So I'm interested in Barry's movements on Monday night,' he said. 'Did you see anything of him ?'

'No. If I had done, I'd tell you,' said Dixie earnestly, and no man on earth could have told that he was not speaking the absolute truth. 'I'd like to help the lad if

I can. If he has an alibi with any of his mates, I'll let you know. A real alibi, I mean.'

'I'll give you your alibi,' said Popsie, staring insolently not at Martineau but at Dixie. 'Barry Hill was with Lennie Leroy. They were in Jimmy Ganders together.'

The tavern known as Jimmy Ganders was a haunt of Dixie's men, but nowadays Dixie considered himself to be too good and too great a man to be seen in such a place. 'What the hell were you doing in that shack ?' he demanded, with heat and force.

'I wasn't in it. I saw them go in, that's all.'

'What time was this ?' Martineau interposed.

'About half-past seven. Don't ask me what time they came out.'

'You were supposed to be at the pictures. You told me you'd been to the pictures,' Dixie accused.

'I did tell you I'd been to the pictures. I didn't tell you what time I came out, though.'

'You're lying, you little tramp !' Dixie raged.

'Ha ha, you're jealous. I've seen you looking at Lennie. You fancy a bit on the side there, don't you ? Well, let me tell you something. Barry Hill has been a freeman of the borough with Lennie for months. She's crackers on him. Oh boy, will there be some trouble when she hears about this McQuade girl. She'll be fit to give somebody the vitriol treatment.'

'And there's been this carry-on right under my nose,' muttered Dixie, as if to himself. 'The boys aren't telling me what goes on.'

'Not the half of it,' Popsie mocked.

Martineau managed to get in another question : 'Where does this Lennie Leroy live ?'

'5D Chatham Street. It's a little flat.'

'See, he knows the address by heart,' came Popsie's gibe.

'I ought to, the whole building is mine,' Dixie snarled. 'My agent let Lennie have that flat.'

Martineau waited for more revelations, but Popsie was silent, smiling in cruel triumph at Dixie. He glowered at her, but he, too, was silent.

The inspector grinned. 'We'd better be going,' he said. 'Then you can fight it out in private.'

He turned and walked out, and Devery followed him. Dixie accompanied them to the street door. 'You see,' he confided, 'if I don't have that floosie out of my house within the week. She's poisonous. I'm not even sure she's true to me.'

'And will you put Miss Leroy in her place ?' Martineau asked.

Dixie gave serious thought to the question. 'Her affair with Barry will be all but bust up,' he said musingly, and then, 'No, dammit ! It's time I had a bit of peace and quiet.'

The two policemen left him then, and when they were in their car Devery remarked, 'You've known Dixie a lot longer than I have. Do you ever find anything likeable about him ?'

'Oh, aye, many a time,' replied his superior, with tolerance. 'They say the devil himself is a likeable fellow.'

'He seems to be a bit more tame, these days.'

'Don't be kidded. Dixie isn't tame, he's just well fed. If it comes to eigh-lads-eigh he'll be just as mean and murderous as ever he was, and just as clever with it. I've never managed to nail him for anything yet. Still, there's time. I have a few more years to serve.'

'He seemed to be helpful enough today.'

'If he was, it was for his own ends,' said Martineau with finality, and Devery thought that he had better say no more about Dixie Costello.

The police car took them to Chatham Street, a thoroughfare of converted Georgian town houses. Number 5D was a third-floor flat. The street door was open. They walked up the stairs.

The name was on the door, on a framed visiting card. 'Miss Lenore Leroy. Commercial Model.'

'It's a good name. I wonder how she came to think of it,' said Devery as Martineau put his thumb on the bell button.

They heard the brisk click of heels on the other side of the door. The handle turned and the door opened wide, and there was Miss Leroy with a hand to her hair and a bright smile on her face. The immediate impression she gave was that she liked to have visitors. She was certainly worth a visit. She was one of those handsome, milky-skinned redheads, and she had the sort of figure people expect a model to have.

Then the smile disappeared as only such smiles can, gone without trace. For a fraction of a second of blank disappointment Miss Leroy showed what she was, an extremely tough baby. Then she was haughty : a lady, apparently, who thought something about herself.

'What is it ?' she wanted to know. And frostily, 'Are you insurance men ?'

'No, ma'am,' said Martineau with humility. 'We're only policemen.'

'And what on earth can you want from me ?'

'Just a word or two of information. May we come in ?'

The look on her face was an insult. She gestured for them to enter.

They walked through a little hallway where small rugs lay thrown apparently at random on polished boards. They entered a small, comfortable living-room. The room had a warm, scented air. They stood with their hats in their hands until she snapped, 'Oh, sit down.' Devery's meek expression was a match for Martineau's. The grin behind it was not discernible.

They sat down. Miss Leroy also took a seat. Martineau said, 'I am making inquiries into the murder of Inspector McQuade. You may have heard of it.'

'Of course. But what on earth has it got to do with me ?'

'That is what I want to find out. Did you ever meet McQuade ?'

'Not to my knowledge.'

'Did you ever meet any of his family ?'

'I didn't even know he had a family.'

'Well, that simplifies matters. Would you like to tell me what you did on Monday evening, and where you went ?'

'I would not. This is silly. I'm not mixed up in any murder case, and I don't intend to be.'

'You can't help it, Miss Leroy,' said Martineau very respectfully. 'At about half-past seven on Monday, were you in the company of a man called Barry Hill ?'

Miss Leroy's milky skin turned pink. 'Yes,' she admitted.

'And did you go with him to a public house called Jimmy Ganders ?'

The girl went pinker still. 'If I did, so what ?' she demanded, merely defiant now. Her air of superiority had taken a bad knock. Jimmy Ganders was notoriously the haunt of women of a certain type, and, moreover, of the rougher sort of that type.

Martineau patiently repeated the question.

'Yes,' she answered reluctantly.

'And how long did you stay there ?'

'Not so long. It's a place I don't much care for.'

'No, I would hardly have thought it was up to your standard,' said Martineau guilefully, and Miss Leroy became visibly less hostile.

'I should say not. Crummy hole,' she replied.

'About how long did you stay ?'

'Three-quarters of an hour. Then I came away.'

'Alone ?'

'Yes. I left him there.'

'May I ask why he took *you* to a place like that ?'

The girl did not miss the implied compliment, and

obviously she liked it. 'He said he had something to talk about,' she replied without hesitation. 'He didn't want to be interrupted by any of my friends.'

'It must have been something important.'

'It was something concerning Barry and me, and nobody else.'

'I see. And did it make you angry ?'

'Why do you say that ?'

'Well, you walked out of the place and left him.'

'Whether I was angry or not is nobody's business but my own. I've told you how long I was with Barry. That's what you wanted, isn't it ?'

'Yes, that's what I wanted. Did you see him again, later ?'

'No. I went straight home, and stayed there.'

'Right. Thank you very much, Miss Leroy.'

'Do you think Barry did the murder ?' the girl asked. She sounded almost hopeful. Obviously she had quarrelled with Hill on Monday night.

'We don't have any opinions yet. While he was with you in Jimmy Ganders, did he talk to anyone else ?'

'No. He nodded to one or two people, that's all,' Miss Leroy replied. Now she seemed to be not unfriendly. She went on, 'You're Martineau, aren't you ?'

'That is my name,' the inspector admitted.

'A lot of folk are scared of you. I'm not.'

'I would not like you to be,' he replied solemnly.

'But you'll bear watching. You're a kidder. That smooth line of yours is all my eye.'

He grinned at her, and merely said, 'May I use your phone ?'

'I have no phone,' she told him.

He believed her. So Dixie Costello could not have telephoned and primed her about what she had to say. It was a reasonable certainty that she had been telling something like the truth. Her evidence was not vital, anyway. It only went to show that Barry Hill's gaming-house alibi had been faked. Why had not Hill told the truth about it ? No doubt because he was afraid that the police would tell Tess McQuade about the other woman in his life.

Martineau thanked Miss Leroy again, and then he and Devery departed. She went with them to the door, and perhaps she listened at the head of the stairs as they went down. But they did not speak until their car was carrying them towards Headquarters, when Martineau said, 'So they had something to talk about.'

Devery nodded. 'Could it be that he wanted to tell her, as gently as possible, that the song was ended but the melody lingered on ?'

'Something like that, I imagine. He gave her a more-or-less polite brush-off, and she didn't like it.'

'I don't suppose he'd be daft enough to mention Tess.'

'No, but La Leroy will soon find out about Tess, if she wants to.'

'All this indicates that Hill is trying to do the right thing by Tess. He's not philandering.'

'No. More's the pity,' said Martineau with a sigh. 'If he was, it would give us an excuse to break the thing up. He's not good enough for Tess.'

They arrived at Headquarters and went into the C.I.D. Cassidy was there, with the lying statements of Waddy, Sloan, Waters and Ricks.

Martineau read them with a faint smile, and threw them down on the desk. The four mobsters had backed up their friend manfully. The statements had not been given on oath, so at that stage there was no question of perjury.

The sergeant who had been in charge of the search of Barry Hill's lodgings was also there to report. He had found a number of offensive weapons, but no firearm of any description. Neither had he found any other sort of evidence. 'I think he must burn every letter he gets,' the sergeant concluded regretfully.

'What did Hill's landlady have to say?' Martineau asked.

'Plenty. She is a woman who likes to look out of the window, and she has an imagination. But the only thing which might be of any use is a tale about a taxi. It was waiting along the street for half-an-hour on Monday night, and she couldn't figure out why.'

'What time?'

'A quarter-to-seven till a quarter-past. She says it moved off when Hill went out, as if it were following him.'

'Was Hill home at a quarter-past seven?' the inspector asked sharply.

'He called home. The landlady says he slipped in quietly and went to his room, and went out again. Then the taxi followed him. She saw the driver, but she couldn't see who the passenger was.'

Martineau thought about the passenger. Who else but Mick McQuade was likely to have been following Hill? And being on his own private inquiry he would use a taxi instead of a plain C.I.D. car.

'Did you get the landlady's statement?' he asked.

'No, sir. She wouldn't give one. When it came to a matter of putting it on paper she took fright.'

'Never mind. Find me the taxi, and the driver. If there's anything in it, his is the statement we want.'

'Verygoodsir,' said the sergeant, and he turned away.

'Now then,' said Martineau to Devery. 'Something to eat, while we've got the chance.'

It was nearly four o'clock, and they were much too late for lunch in the police canteen. They went out to a little restaurant where they were well known, and persuaded the proprietor to persuade his chef to grill some steak for them. They ate the steak, and returned to Headquarters full of beef. Martineau went along to Superintendent Clay's office.

He knocked and entered. The chief of the C.I.D. was sitting behind his desk. He stared at his subordinate in his usual way, as if he had never seen him before, then he said, 'Well, what goes on ?'

He listened in silence while Martineau told him about the happenings of the day, then he commented, 'So you've done much work, but gathered very few potatoes.'

'That's about it, sir,' Martineau admitted.

'Never mind. Leave no stone unturned. And by the way, I've got some bad news for you. Your Assize job is off.'

'Which one. Do you mean Leon Crow ?'

'Yes.'

'How can it be off ?'

'Because he's dead. He was killed on a pedestrian crossing in Spring Street just before noon, the busiest time of the day.'

'What killed him ?'

'Nothing doing. It was a corporation bus.'

'All right. What were the circumstances ?'

'Apparently the bus driver didn't have a chance. There was a P.C. controlling the crossing. He'd stopped all pedestrians and he was letting traffic through. There was a crowd of pedestrians at the kerb, and Crow was in the front rank, right on the kerb. Two buses, one behind the other, were passing at a fair clip close to the kerb. Crow teetered off the kerb and fell in front of the second bus. A wheel went over him.'

'Any witnesses ?'

'Plenty. But no real good ones. They're full of opinions, and most of them seem to think that the slipstream of the first bus made Crow lose his balance.'

'What is the P.C.'s opinion ?'

'He hasn't got one. He couldn't see for traffic.'

'What is *your* opinion, sir ?'

'I wasn't there, was I ? *Nobody* saw Crow pushed, if that's on your mind.'

'No evidence of foul play whatsoever, then ?'

'None. I have all the reports and statements here. You

can take them away and read them if you like. So far as I can see, the verdict at the inquest will be based on the evidence, and it will be a verdict of accidental death. I shall let it go at that. I have no option.'

'But if the inquest produces any evidence ?'

'That will be different. But as it stands it's an accident. I'm not going to try to make a murder case out of a job we wouldn't clear in a thousand years. I have enough uncleared murders, thank you.'

Martineau nodded. The coincidence of Crow's death was a cause for suspicion, but there was no evidence. They had enough uncleared murders, so why try to make another one ?

10

JULIA MARTINEAU was a tall, elegant woman, urban to
the backbone, but she would have suffered no hardship in
keeping the hours of a farmer's wife. Regularly she opened
her eyes at the crack of dawn, and lay in bed wakeful for
an hour or more before light slumber came to rest her
until getting-up time. On the morning of Sunday, the sixth
day after the murder of Mick McQuade, she was awake
long before daylight, and she was waiting for the first
suburban backyard cock to crow when she heard unmistakably, through the open bedroom window, the familiar
click of the latch of her own front gate.

Puzzled, she raised her head from the pillow and
listened. Stealthy noises came to her ears. One of them
was a faint metallic knock which sounded to her very much
as if someone had gently put down a bin or a big can.
Then there was a noise which she associated with the front
door ; a fumbling with the lock or the letter-box. In the
stillness of the serene small hours the sounds were faint,
but definite.

She was not a timid woman and she did not immediately
rouse her husband. Before doing that, she wanted to see
for herself. She slipped out of bed and went to the window.
She lifted the light curtain aside and looked out. There
was a car without lights standing in the road near the gate,
and its two kerb-side doors were hanging open. She pro-
truded her head and looked down. At the door was the
thickset figure of a man, and he was crouching at the

letter-box, which was not a box at all but merely a slot with a hinged metal cover. Near to the man was an upright cylinder about two feet high, and there appeared to be a pipe from the cylinder to the door. There was a distinct hissing sound. The man appeared to be squirting something through the letter-box.

Julia withdrew from the window. She went to the bedroom door and opened it. As she did so she smelled petrol, lots of petrol. The air of the stairs and landing was heavy with the odour.

She knew what that meant, and she knew that the flow of petrol had to be stopped at once. She switched on the landing light, and stepped forward to look down the stairs. She could see the front door and the letter-box, and the brass nozzle which was sticking through the slot. The nozzle was pointing upward and moving from side to side, and from it came a coarse spray of liquid on to the hallway and stairs.

She saw that only for a second, and then the spray stopped and the nozzle was withdrawn. She knew then how much time she had ; just the time it takes a man to strike a match. She screamed, but she also acted without hesitation. The scream was intended to awaken her sleeping husband, the action was to go into the back bedroom to her child. With the deft movements of a mother she threw aside bedclothes and gathered up the three-year-old, and as she did so she realized that she would not have time to get back to the other room. She slammed the door of the bedroom, and not a moment too soon.

Martineau was awakened suddenly and completely by his wife's scream. He heard the door of the child's bedroom as it was slammed, and he knew what that was. Then there was dull thunder as the explosive outburst of fire and the roar of flames merged into one sound. A sheet of flame roared up the stairs and in scarcely any time at all was halfway across the landing. He scrambled out of bed and closed the bedroom door. In sheer self-preservation it was the only thing to do.

He switched on the bedroom light. It burned just long enough to show him that he was alone in the room, and then it went out. He stood still for a moment as conjecture raced through his mind. His first thought was that Julia had gone downstairs to make herself a hot drink, and had somehow started a terrible fire. Then he remembered the scream, which he could have sworn was uttered quite near him. Then he remembered the slamming of a bedroom door. Were Julia and the child both in the back bedroom ? He hoped so, he fervently hoped so.

But he was not sure, and he had to be sure. He had to get into the back bedroom. He opened his door, and closed it quickly. The door itself was already burning, and beyond it was a furnace. He could not possibly go through six feet of searing flame to get to the door of the child's room.

What could he do ? Break down the wall between the two rooms ? He suddenly realized that he might be able to do that very thing, and he blessed the thrifty contractor who had specified cheap coke-breeze and plaster instead of honest brick for that interior wall. Coughing from the smoke which now filled his room, he groped for the heavy stool which was beside Julia's dressing-table. He attacked the wall with the stool.

He smashed the stool. When he had dropped it in pieces he felt at the wall, and found that it was slightly concave at the place where he had been hitting it. The heat in the room was terrible, and he could hardly breathe for smoke. The panels of the door were burned through, and there was some fiery, smoky light in the room. He knew that he had not much time ; only a few seconds before the smoke and the heat overcame him. He turned and picked up the tallboy, a smallish one weighing about fifty pounds. He used it like a battering ram, striking the breeze wall with its sharp upper corner. It made a hole in the wall at the first attempt. He banged away frantically with the thing until he had made a hole big enough to tumble head first through. He saw that the back room was in better condition than his own. It was not so smoky, and he could see the silhouette of Julia at the window. He bellowed at her, a strangled shout which came between coughs. He did not want her to drop little Susan on to the concrete at the backyard, or even to jump with her. Both of them would be better at the front, dropping on to the kindlier surface of a lawn which needed mowing.

He saw Julia's head move, and he made out the shape of the child in her arms. She had heard his voice, but she could not understand how it came to be in the room.

'Julia !' he yelled. 'Here ! There's a way out !'

She heard him, and she came to him. He pulled the child through the hole, and took her to the open window. He went back for Julia, and found her halfway through. He pulled her through also.

'Now then,' he shouted in her ear. 'I'll go through first, then you'll drop Susan to me. Then you'll drop. The lawn won't hurt you.'

He got through the window and hung for a moment by his hands before he dropped on to the lawn. He turned, holding out his hands for Susan. But the crying, terrified little girl clung to her mother. Julia had to be ruthless and tear the little arms from around her neck before she could get the child out of the window. She had to smack the little hands which clung desperately to her nightdress, her fingers, anything. When Susan dropped she came down awkwardly, spreadeagled, but Martineau caught her. He sat her down on the lawn and let her howl, and as he did so, help arrived.

It was the policeman on the beat, out of breath. 'I saw the blaze and called the Fire Brigade, sir,' he said.

As he spoke he looked up at Julia, as did Martineau. She had somehow managed to get both feet out of the window, and she was sitting on the sill. She seemed afraid to jump, and unable to make the turn to get into a position to drop.

'What about my cape, sir ?' said the P.C., taking the folded mass of thick blue melton from his shoulder. 'It'll break her fall a bit.'

A policeman's cape is almost as big as a blanket. The two men held the cape, leaning back to achieve maximum tautness. 'Jump !' shouted Martineau.

Julia jumped, and even in that dire situation she remembered her modesty. She held her nightdress tightly round her legs with one hand. She landed feet first on the middle of the cape. The others were pulled down. All three of them went down on the lawn, but none of them were hurt. Julia sprang up and ran to her child.

The Fire Brigade arrived. It was obvious that they could not save the house, but they poured water into it with the intention of saving the semi-detached house which was its neighbour.

Martineau and his wife stood for a little while on the extreme edge of the lawn, watching the fire. He held the child, who no longer cried, and he had one arm to spare to put around Julia's shoulders. She wept bitterly, and she was a woman who seldom cried. Her home, the little home she loved, wantonly sent up in flames. That was too much for her.

Martineau was bitter, too, for his wife's grief, for the danger in which she and the child had been, for his piano and his beloved records. And all he knew just yet was that it was no accident. One broken-hearted outburst by Julia had told him that. 'All right, Mr. Bashful,' he breathed fiercely. 'You're playing for keeps now, and so am I. No mercy, Bashful. No mercy.'

Daylight was coming. A cock crowed. Lights were showing in a number of houses on the suburban road, for the various noises of fire and fire-fighting had awakened other neighbours. Martineau and his family were taken indoors. They were given coffee laced with spirit, warm blankets and dressing-gowns, warm slippers for their feet. Susan and Julia went to bed. Martineau had a hot bath, and then he went to Headquarters in an overcoat too small, trousers too short, borrowed socks and carpet slippers.

He had heard the full story from Julia, and he had blessed her for her wakefulness and her promptitude. He knew now that Bashful or his emissary was a thickset man of middle height. This man, he thought, was probably Bashful himself. He had a dark-coloured, medium-sized car. The equipment he had used to spray petrol into Martineau's house was probably one of those cylinders which fruit farmers strapped to their backs when they wanted to walk around spraying their trees. No doubt Bashful had used the coarsest nozzle which the makers supplied, because he had spread around quite a lot of petrol in a little time. If he had been allowed to empty his cylinder, the consequent rush of flame would have been such that nobody could have got out of the house alive. The spray equipment provided a line of inquiry if it had been newly acquired for the purpose of roasting Martineau, but more probably it had already been in Bashful's possession. That led to the assumption that Bashful had a house or estate of considerable size in the country or the outer suburbs, with a big garden and an orchard. Or else he had stolen the equipment from such a house.

The reason why Julia had not heard the approach of Bashful's car was easily found. Martineau's house was on a slight incline. The car had coasted down to it in neutral gear. Bashful had opened doors to get himself and his equipment out, and he had left them open. Only the click of the gate had advertised his approach to the house. Every time Martineau thought of that he expelled a breath of relief. He had been incredibly lucky.

By eight o'clock he was weary of tight trousers. He

telephoned Maxim's Stores, and his call was answered by a watchman. The watchman gave him the manager's name and phone number, and he called the manager. This man, Mr. Danski, was still in bed when his phone rang, and his answer was somewhat ill-humoured. But when Martineau had introduced himself and explained his predicament, he became actively sympathetic. 'I'll attend to the matter myself,' he said. 'I'll meet you at the store in an hour.'

So, shortly after nine o'clock that morning the Martineau family, looking rather like the survivors of a shipwreck, entered the big store and began to choose new clothes. This proceeding made Julia moderately happy, and the sight of her happiness heartened Martineau. He told her to buy whatever she liked ; they had money in the bank. Even Maxim's did not have much choice in ready-made clothes in his size, but he found a suit in a nice West of England cloth which fitted him quite well.

From Maxim's, Julia and Susan and two suitcases full of new clothes went to Julia's mother's house, and Martineau went back to work. He found Headquarters in a moderate hubbub of excitement. Men looked at him curiously as he went through to the C.I.D. Devery was waiting for him, his superintendent wanted to see him, and the Chief Constable, having been informed, also wanted to see him. He said, 'All right,' and went into his own office. There was one thing worrying him. He looked up the telephone number of the local manager of the company which carried his fire insurance. He called the man and told him about the fire. He was told that he need not worry about his claim. Greatly comforted, he went to see Clay.

Clay took him to the Chief. He had to tell his tale again. The two senior officers listened in horror and amazement. When he had done, the Chief exploded into comment. Never in all his career, etc. He also offered sympathy and help. In the presence of the Old Man, Clay said nothing, but his face showed his feelings. From that moment on, Martineau was going to have all the men and the help he requested in his search for Bashful.

The inspector returned to the C.I.D. At a nod from him, Devery followed him into his office. The two men looked at each other. 'I'm told it was a very close call, sir,' the sergeant said.

'Middling close,' Martineau agreed.

'Bashful is getting real rough.'

'Yes. I think, when we get hold of him, we'll find he's slightly crackers. I don't think any man in his right mind would have done what he did this morning.'

'He must feel that we're getting near to him.'

'Yes, but *how* are we getting nearer to him. We don't know a thing.'

Devery thought about that. 'Yesterday there were some new faces in the picture,' he said. 'Hill, Costello, Costello's mob. Popsie and Lennie Leroy.'

'And Tess McQuade. But we've more-or-less eliminated Hill from the job, and the others only came into it through him.'

'Nevertheless, Bashful immediately starts getting real tough. There may be a connection somewhere.'

'Well,' said Martineau, 'I don't see it yet. But between Bashful and the murderer of Mick McQuade I can see a connection, all right. The man who put Mick away is trying to put me away, and for the same reason.'

'We've turned up every job McQuade had since he transferred from Liverpool City into this force. We didn't get a lead there.'

Martineau shook his head. 'I knew Mick when he was in Liverpool City,' he said reminiscently. 'I helped him once with a prisoner.' Suddenly he jerked erect in his chair. 'Hell's bells !'

'Thought of something, sir ?' Devery wanted to know.

'Yes. There is one certain man. I don't know where

he is today, but McQuade and I were probably the only men in Granchester who knew him by sight. And he was a stockbroker I Claude Jackman. Ever heard of him ?'

'Can't say I have.'

'Well, you ought to have. He's still a badly wanted man. He's been wanted for years and years.'

'Before my time, perhaps.'

'Yes, before your time. Twelve or thirteen years ago. I remember that day as if it were yesterday. I got commended. I was a D.O. at that time, and I went over to Liverpool to try and get some admissions from an itinerant housebreaker they'd caught. I'd just got outside Lime Street Station when I saw a uniform man having a hell of a fight with a civvy. Naturally I went and helped the P.C., who was none other than McQuade, then a stranger to me. This fellow he had was as strong as a bull, but we got the snaps on him and locked him up. He was Claude Jackman.'

'And his offence ?'

'At that time every policeman in England was looking for him. He was a London stockbroker who was able to diddle his clients long enough to scarper with a fortune of their money. The only case of its kind I ever heard of. Well, he went to Liverpool, and McQuade nailed him. But he didn't have the money with him. He'd sided that somewhere. It was never found.'

'What did the judge give him ?'

'Fourteen years. But he didn't serve six months. I've heard it said that he had his escape organized before he went in. Anyway, he got away and he's never been heard of since.'

'Which prison ?'

'The Moor. He's the only one who ever got out and stayed out.'

'And you'd know him again ?'

'Would I I I'll never forget the look he gave me when

they were taking him down to the cells. As poisonous as hell.'

'What was he like, physically ?'

'A good-looking bloke. Short curly hair, reddish brown. Thirty-five years old I think he was at that time. Medium height. Very thick neck and strong shoulders. Powerful. Anyway, you can look at his picture. He'll still be in the files of the *Police Gazette*.'

'It's worth going into, sir. You very seldom get stock-brokers having trouble with the police. And yet McQuade was investigating the affairs of a stockbroker, and now this other geezer's name crops up in connection with him.'

Martineau became thoughtful. There was a hard glint in his eye. 'Also,' he said, 'according to Julia the character who set fire to my house was a heavy-built fellow. Go and see what we've got on Jackman. I'll feast my eyes on that mug again.'

Devery went, and Martineau waited, musing. Jackman. Was it possible ? Could he have been hiding here in Granchester all these years ? Living the life of Riley and dabbling in stocks and shares ?

He thought once more about the Bassey case. All the people involved had been seen by himself or McQuade. Except two. Eugene Drax, who was supposed to be fishing in Scotland, and William Taylor, who was supposed to be in London. Could either of those two be Claude Jackman ?

Devery returned, looked pleased with himself. 'I didn't need to bother with the *Gazette*, sir,' he said. 'We have a file on him. I found it in the Wanted box, right at the back.'

He put the file on the desk and opened it as a rare book dealer might open a treasured folio. He stared at the three excellent photographs ; full length, full face, and profile.

It was a well-dressed man, of medium height as des-cribed and handsome as Martineau had said. Devery, who was one of those people who like to see animal likenesses in human faces, was struck by Jackman's resemblance to

114

a bull. The forehead was low and wide, topped by close curls. The eyes were hot and dark, the nose short with flared nostrils. The lips and chin were the best part of the picture, showing considerable resolution and betraying no weakness. The neck was powerful. The whole face glowered. Overbearing arrogance was its characteristic.

'That's him all right,' said Martineau. 'I'd know him anywhere.'

'My word, I think I would, too,' said Devery thoughtfully.

II

DEVERY WAS STILL GAZING at Claude Jackman's photograph when there came a knock on the door. Martineau called 'Come in,' and a plain clothes man entered. It was the detective sergeant who had directed the search of Barry Hill's lodgings.

'I found your cab driver, sir,' he said. 'The one who followed Hill. His passenger was Inspector McQuade, all right. He identified him from his photograph. I stuck it in the rogues' book and let him turn the pages. He had no hesitation when he saw it.'

'Hadn't he already recognized Inspector McQuade from his picture in the paper?' Martineau queried.

'He says not, sir. Sometimes newspaper photos aren't very good. Also the inspector had given him the wrong idea altogether. Hill met a young woman at Somerset Square, and when they walked away the inspector paid off the cab and followed them. The driver thought it was some sort of man-and-wife job, with McQuade as the jealous husband.'

'I see. Well, he must be certain of his man if he picked him out of the book.'

'Yes, sir. Do you want to see him?'

'No. Get his statement, and get your times right.'

'Yessir.' The sergeant departed.

'So now we're an hour further on,' said Martineau. 'We can assume that McQuade saw Hill and Leroy go

116

into Jimmy Ganders at about half-past seven. And so did Popsie. I wonder if Popsie spotted McQuade.'

'Would she know him ?'

'She might. She's knocked about with Dixie Costello long enough to have had him pointed out to her.'

'If she knew McQuade, she may have waited to see what happened.'

'And that being so, she should know whether or not Mick followed Hill when he came out of the pub.'

'Do we interrogate Popsie ?'

'We certainly do, when we get the chance. But we don't want Dixie around,' said Martineau. He stretched himself and yawned. 'We know a little more than we did. It's almost a certainty that Mick was wise to Hill and Tess, and he was playing it crafty. He was trying to get something on Hill so that he could break the thing up.'

'And when he saw Hill meet Leroy, he'd think he'd got what he wanted.'

'Yes, he'd think young Barry was two-timing.'

'So instead of following Hill from Jimmy Ganders, he might have followed Leroy, to find out who she was and where she lived.'

'Yes, if he didn't know that already. It's a possibility we must bear in mind,' said the chief inspector. He looked at his watch. 'After all the trouble I've been through I'm entitled to a drink. If we walk from here to the Northland it'll be well turned opening time.' He grinned. 'We'll give you another chance to make it up with Ella.'

Devery had no reply to that. He picked up his hat as he followed Martineau through the main office, and they walked to the Northland Hotel.

Ella's bar was a popular Sunday lunch-time meeting place. She was already moderately busy, but not too busy to see the two detectives as they entered. Her eyes sought Devery's face, reading his expression almost with anxiety, and then she smiled.

Martineau ordered a pint of bitter ; Devery said that
he would have a half-pint. Ella drew the beer and, instead
of putting it before them, she put it on the bar near the
end and waited for them to go to her. They moved
obediently, and by doing so they put a little distance
between themselves and their nearest neighbours at the
bar.

'What's all this about, Ella ?' Martineau queried jovially.
'Have you got something to tell us ?'

She smiled almost demurely, and her glance flashed to
Devery's face before she answered Martineau. 'What is it
you want to know ?' she asked.

'Just tell us who did it, that's all. That's the one tiny
clue we need to clear any crime.'

She shook her head. 'Gossip is what I've got.'

'Concerning whom ?'

'A very old friend of yours. Mr. District of Columbia.'

That beat Martineau. He did not know anybody called
Washington. He looked at Devery. The sergeant shook his
head.

Then it came to Martineau. Dixie Costello, of course.
'I get you,' he said. 'What's the griff ?'

Ella's glance again flashed to Devery. This was his information, really. She was trying to please him, to get back
on to some sort of friendly footing with him.

'There was one hell of a schemozzle in here last night,'
she said. 'A lady who shall be nameless got herself paralytic.
She became offensive. She made a fool of the great I Am,
and the great I Am was annoyed, to put it mildly. Especially
so since there was another lady—almost a real lady, by the
look of her—giving him the admiring eye on the sly. So
he called his minions and had the offending baggage removed. To the York Road Hotel, I heard him say, just
so that she had a bed for the night. She left her handbag
on the bar. The Sublime Ego opened the bag and took out

a key, and put it in his pocket. Then he sent the bag after the baggage.'

Smiling sweetly then, Ella moved away to serve a customer. Martineau grinned at his companion. 'That's just to show you she may be an honest barmaid, but never a higgerent one,' he said. 'So Dixie turned the fair Popsie out of house and home. Interesting, very.'

Devery nodded absently. He was looking at Ella. He was looking at Ella as if he had just seen her for the first time.

Ella served several customers, and then she returned. Martineau said, 'All right. Now give us Part Two of this enthralling serial.'

'Part Two,' said Ella solemnly. 'When the wicked sorceress had been driven from the stage, the noble knight started to woo the lady fair. He did not have any hard going with that, because the lady met him more than halfway. From the silly look on his face, she was using butter by the pound.'

'Did he go out with her ?'

'He did. Or maybe she went out with him.'

'So, he's got himself a new sweetheart,' said Martineau thoughtfully. 'What's she like ?'

'A tall blonde. She looks like money to me. Mint condition, too.'

'Is that so ?' said the inspector, but without much interest. His thoughts had turned from the new girl to the old one. He could not see Popsie tamely accepting dismissal to an hotel room, unless she were too drunk to know what was happening. 'Excuse me,' he said. 'I'll be back in a minute.'

He went to the hotel lounge, where there was a public telephone box. He called Police Headquarters, and asked for the superintendent in charge of the uniform branch. His call was put through.

'You're just in time,' said the superintendent, who

119

normally worked only a half-day on Sunday. 'I was nearly away home.'

'I won't keep you a minute, sir,' said Martineau. 'You will have seen all last night's reports, I suppose ?'

'Yes.'

'Was there anything from the vicinity of All Saints Road ?'

'There was. I suppose you're referring to Dixie Costello's bit of stuff. She was arrested.'

'What's the story ?'

'The man on the beat found her banging and kicking at Costello's door at one-fifteen. She was drunk. She told him she'd lost her key and was locked out. The P.C. did a bit of banging himself, and Costello opened a bedroom window. The P.C.—a youngster called Emerson—told him to come down and let his wife in. Dixie said, "She's not my wife and she doesn't live here." The woman, Violet Bootle alias Popsie, pulled off one of her shoes and threw it at him. She used some atrocious language. She also told Emerson that Costello was keeping all her clothes. Costello said, "All her clothes are at the York Road Hotel and she has a room there. You make inquiries there, Constable, and you'll find that what I say is true." Then he shut the window.'

'The end of the affair,' said Martineau.

'Not so far as the police are concerned, it isn't. Emerson suggested that she should go to the York Road Hotel and verify Costello's story. He even offered to go with her. She really let herself go then, screaming and yelling the obscene stuff. Emerson locked her up. She was bailed out this morning by a woman called Anita Crawford. Another old bag.'

Before the end of the story Martineau was ready with his plea. 'Listen, sir,' he said. 'I have an idea that this woman might have some information about the McQuade job. It might be valuable information, it might not. Could I

120

offer her something ? Even a complete let-off if necessary ?'

'The McQuade job is a lot more important than cooling off Violet Bootle,' said the superintendent, who knew as much about Misdemeanour and Compounding Offences as did Clay of the C.I.D. 'I daresay you could offer her a let-off, but not on my authority. You'll have to go higher than me.'

'With your permission, sir, I'll do that.'

'Permission granted, and the best of luck,' said the superintendent.

Martineau returned to Ella's bar. Ella was busy. Devery was watching her. He was watching her with such interest that he did not immediately notice his superior's return.

'Snap out of it,' said the latter, in good humour. 'We've got work to do.'

'Yes, sir,' said Devery, not startled at all. 'Before we go, would you like to take a look at Dixie's new sweetie. He's just gone into the cocktail bar with her.'

'I wouldn't call it important, but I may as well,' said the inspector. He strode out, and crossed the lounge to the doorway of the cocktail bar. He looked in. He saw Costello, deep in conversation with Sylvia Paris. He turned and walked back to Devery.

'That's the woman who puts fivers in your hat,' he said. 'I hope Dixie doesn't take her for too much.'

Devery stared. 'How the dickens has she got mixed up with him ?' he wanted to know.

'I mentioned his name to her. I also told her to keep away from him. Of course I might have known she'd do nothing of the kind.'

'What does she want from him ?'

'Set a thief to catch a thief is the idea. Come on, let's go.'

They waved a casual farewell to Ella and went out. In the street, Martineau stopped and said, 'Popsie was locked up last night for using the wrong words to a P.C. I'm going to try and get permission to trade a let-off for information, if she has any. At this moment she'll probably be taking nourishment somewhere. You nose around the likely places and see if you can locate her.'

'That I'll do, sir,' said Devery cheerfully. They parted, and the sergeant strolled along to the Stag Hotel. He thought about Popsie. He supposed that she would go back whence she came, to the streets. But not yet. First she would try to find herself another protector, someone to keep her in idleness and luxury. If she had already begun to operate on that project, then she would be in one of the town's better hotels.

Popsie was not in the Stag. She was not in the Queen's. She was not in the Grand. She was not in the County. In search of her, Devery also went into the Royal Lancaster, but only because he was passing the place. The Royal Lancs was the sort of hotel where a British waiter would be a pariah. It was Swiss managed, French served, French valeted. It was the hostelry of visiting notables. Everything eaten or drunk there was of the best, and it also cost three times as much as it was worth. Devery did not expect to find Popsie in that place.

She was there, gracing the cocktail bar. She was alone and she looked bored. There were not many people in the bar ; only the white-coated barman ; Popsie sitting on a bar stool ; two men at a table, looking serious enough to be discussing business ; two smart women at another table, looking avid enough to be discussing someone else's business ; nobody else.

Devery walked to the bar and stood about four feet away from Popsie. She lounged round-backed on her stool, and in consequence of this and the cut of her dress a good deal of her adequate frontal development was visible. Devery had eyes to see, but he also had control of them. He seemed not to have noticed the girl. He ordered a gin and tonic, and then he looked up to meet a baleful stare.

'This just makes it perfect,' said Popsie. 'It isn't enough for the place to be dead. The bloody coppers have to walk in.'

'Hush,' Devery chided gently. 'That sort of talk won't do in here. This is the Royal Lancaster, you know. You mustn't say "bloody coppers". Say "perishing policemen".'

'I didn't know they'd allow a copper in here, anyway.'

'Coppers are allowed anywhere. But I'm surprised that *you* got past the hall porter.'

'Listen, flatfoot,' said Popsie. She was a fervent movie fan, and her idiom was, she believed, modern American. 'Listen, I go anywhere I like, see ? I spend more dough in a month than you see in a year.'

'What's money got to do with it ?' Devery retorted, deliberately not trying to conciliate the girl, because conciliation was not his way with her type. 'What matters in a place like this is whether you're a lady or not.'

'Are you making out I'm not a lady ?'

'I never actually said so, did I ?'

'You as good as said so.'

'Did I ?' Devery seemed to be surprised.

'Yes, you did.'

'Well, are you ?'

That made Popsie pause. 'I'm as good as you, any day,' she said after some thought.

'That can only be a matter of opinion. What will you have to drink ?'

'I don't drink with coppers.'

'Why not ?'

'Because I don't like 'em.'

'Why don't you like them ?'

'Because they're a lot of nosy bastards.'

'Only because it's their job. Outside of that, they're just like anybody else. Take me, for instance——'

'I wouldn't take you with a pension.'

'Take me, for instance,' Devery went on imperturbably.

'I couldn't care less about you and your affairs. If you won't have a drink with me, that's quite all right. What does it matter to me ? You're not my girl, you're Dixie Costello's.'

'I'll have a Martini,' said Popsie suddenly, 'and to hell with Dixie Costello.'　.

'Waiter, two Martinis, please,' said Devery.

'Dixie Costello is the king of all pigs,' said Popsie.

'I believe every word you say,' came the solemn answer.

'He wants that Leroy woman, and she's wagging her backside at him for all she's worth.'

Devery realized that Popsie did not know of the existence of Sylvia Paris. Neither was she aware that Devery knew of her break with Costello. He did not enlighten her on either point.

'You're the woman between,' he encouraged.

'You said it. And I stay between. I'll upset the apple cart.'

'I don't see how you can stop Dixie from going after Leroy, if he makes up his mind.'

'That's because you don't know what day it is. You coppers don't know anything. That woman has a bloke, a rich bloke. She's had this bloke all the time she's been carrying on with Barry Hill. Dixie don't know that— yet.'

'You think that will put him off the girl ?'

'I don't know,' said Popsie. Her eyes narrowed cunningly. She leered, if an undoubtedly handsome girl could be said to leer. 'It'll help. And it'll help a lot more if Leroy gets sent to gaol for life.'

Devery was really startled. 'Whatever for ?'

'You're investigating a murder, aren't you ? Well, investigate Lennie Leroy.'

'But she didn't even know Inspector McQuade.'

'Didn't she ? She was with him last Monday night, anyway.'

'She was ?'

'She got into a taxi with him, just round the corner from Jimmy Ganders.'

'You're sure ?'

'Course I'm sure. I was watching. He waited for her to come out of the pub, after Barry Hill had gone. He went and spoke to her, raising his hat very polite. They walked off together and then there was this taxi. He flagged it and they got in. I was watching all the time.'

'You're a clever girl, aren't you ?'

'I know what's going on,' said Popsie with satisfaction. She drank her Martini.

'Have another,' Devery urged.

'Yes, I will. Order it while I go and powder my nose, will you ? Excuse me.'

She picked up her small, smart handbag and slipped her tidily rounded buttocks from the bar stool. She walked out of the bar. Devery ordered another Martini for her, and then he went in search of a telephone. He called Headquarters, and asked for Martineau. The inspector came on the line. 'It's about time you rang in,' he grumbled.

'How did you go on, sir ?' Devery wanted to know.

'All right. I got clearance. All I want now is the girl.'

'I've got her here, at the Royal Lancs. She's talking freely. She's just gone to the Ladies, so I took the opportunity to phone you.'

'Get her to come here, if you can. Take a cab.'

'Very good, sir. Now I must get back to the bar.'

He returned to the cocktail bar and waited for Popsie. He waited for fifteen minutes, but she did not return. He began to sip the drink which he had ordered for her. He reflected that it was characteristic of Popsie to walk out like that. She was unpredictable, irresponsible, wanton, spiteful, jealous, vain, and probably untruthful. He hoped that she had not been lying to him. He thought that she had not, even though she had given her information not to help him but to hurt Lennie Leroy.

He looked at his watch. Popsie would be in another bar somewhere, looking pleased with herself. She would think that she had scored off the police by getting Devery to order her a drink while she walked out on him. In a way she had scored off him. She had got away from him by using one of the oldest and simplest tricks in the book. He grinned and shook his head. He finished Popsie's Martini and went to report that he had lost the girl but got the information.

12

DEVERY FOUND MARTINEAU pacing about his office, five steps one way, five the other. 'Well,' demanded the inspector. 'Where is she ?'

'I lost her, sir,' said Devery. He did not seem to be greatly perturbed about that, and the other man, knowing him well, withheld reproof until he had heard the whole story.

Devery told it briefly. 'I imagine we don't need to do a deal with her,' he concluded. 'I think we've got all she knew about McQuade and Leroy. When they went off in a taxi it's hardly likely that she got another taxi and followed. She wouldn't be *that* interested.'

'Perhaps you're right,' Martineau admitted. 'But I'll see her later if I have time.' He was pacing about again, more concerned with the matter of McQuade and Leroy than with Violet Bootle, alias Popsie.

In a little while he stopped. 'First, we want that taxi driver,' he said.

'Yes. And that makes two drivers who carried McQuade on the day of the murder, and kept quiet about it. I'll say that's damn funny.'

Martineau nodded. He thought about the Granchester which he knew as his beat, his range, his parish. The very heart of the city. The small throbbing heart of a big city and a ring of suburbs and satellites with a total population of several millions. The anonymous millions were the life-blood which flowed through the city's heart like so many minute corpuscles. Thousands of those millions made their livelihoods in the city's centre, but they, too, usually remained anonymous. Among those thousands were the true denizens of the city, the comparatively few who knew each other and knew what was going on. These were the hotel keepers and their staffs, the newsboys, the taxi drivers and, to some extent, the bus drivers, the porters and commissionaires, the postmen, the waiters and restaurant-keepers and some of the shopkeepers. This nucleus had a soiled fringe of bookie's runners, prostitutes, whoremongers, thieves and mobsters, queer fellows, bar flies and layabouts. High and low, respectable and disreputable, the denizens of the city's heart knew each other. Many of them knew every policeman of the Headquarters division. And the police knew them. The police knew all of them.

But of those people, the taxi drivers were the most knowing. The life of the day and the life of the night they saw. They observed, and they remembered. Nine out of ten of them had known exactly who and what McQuade was. It was indeed strange that both of the drivers who had picked him up on the night of the murder had remained silent.

'We may get an explanation when we find our man,' he said, and he looked round for his hat. 'We'll have something to eat, and then we'll make a start.'

During the meal he apportioned duties. He told Devery to take a car and go round all the cab ranks in the city. His own intention was to canvass the big taxi firms, and since most of those firms had their head offices in and around Bishopsgate, he would go on foot.

So, after the meal they separated. Martineau walked the short distance to Bishopsgate and started his enquiries there. The first firm he went to was the biggest, the Blue-line Taxi Company. Though it was Sunday, the manager was there. He knew Martineau, and Martineau knew him. When he was told the nature of the enquiry he produced

128

the soiled pencilled scrawls which were last Monday's
journey sheets. On one of them he found an entry which
appeared to be the one required. Two fares had been
picked up in Lacy Street at 8.20 p.m. and taken to Chatham
Street.

'That'll be the one,' said Martineau, pleased with this
early success. 'How can I get hold of the driver ?'

'Easy,' said the manager with quiet pride. 'The police
aren't the only people who have radio cars.'

He opened a hatchway to an adjoining office and said,
'Tell Steelband to come in. I want to see him.' Then
he turned to Martineau, 'Would you like a cup of tea,
Inspector. There may be a few minutes' wait.'

They waited, and drank tea. Then Steelband arrived.
He was a round-shouldered but lithe Jamaican, as black
as the ace of spades. His name, he admitted, was Reginald
Rington, and he had been driving a taxi in Granchester
for only four months. He was nervous, afraid of trouble,
but the manager soon put him at his ease.

'The police need your help, Steelband,' he said kindly.
'Just tell the inspector the exact truth. That's all he wants.'

Martineau brought out McQuade's photograph. 'Have
you ever seen this man ?' he asked.

'Yes, sir,' said Steelband, in the peculiar accent of his
native island. 'He is the police inspector who has been in
all the papers.'

'Yes, but have you ever seen the man himself ?'

Steelband's hesitation was brief. He swallowed, and
then he said, 'Yes, sir. I seen him.'

'When ?'

'Monday night, about twenty-past eight. In Lacy Street,
near Union Street. He got into my taxi with a young lady.'

'Would you know the young lady again ?'

'I would, sure. She was awful pretty.'

'Where did you take these two people ?'

'Chatham Street. Number five.'

'You have a good memory. Did they both alight at number five ?'

'No, sir. The girl alighted and said "Good night," and the gentleman stayed in the cab.'

'And where did you take him then ?'

'Nowhere. Along the street, that's all. He told me to take him to Shirwell, but when we had gone maybe a quarter of a mile he tapped on the dividing window and said something I didn't catch. I slid the window open and he said, "Turn round quick. Follow that car." That was a black Rover which had just passed us, going the other way. I don't remember the number. I slowed and turned like he said, but by the time I'd got round and going again the car was stopping near number five. A man got out and went into the house there. I think it was number five, but I was too far off to be certain.'

'Can you describe the man ?'

Steelband shook his head. 'Too far off, sir. And it had started to go dark. He was nippy on his feet, I can say that. He wasn't in sight more'n a second or two.'

'So what did you do ?'

'I drove on past the car. Some way past, my fare told me to stop. He sat looking out of the back window for a while, then he got out of the cab and paid me.'

'And you drove off and left him there ?'

Steelband rolled his eyes uneasily in the direction of the manager. 'Yes, sir,' he said.

For the first time, Martineau detected something wrong with the man. His early nervousness had passed, and he had been answering questions in a confident way. Now, suddenly, he was nervous again.

Martineau frowned. He stroked his chin. He looked very grave. 'Rington,' he said. 'Have you just told me a lie ?'

Steelband looked miserably at the floor. 'Yes, sir,' he replied.

'How many lies have you told me, altogether ?'

'Just one. Only one.'

'All right. Go back to where you told the lie, and give me the truth.'

The coloured man looked at the manager again, and then he said, 'He got out of the cab and paid me, and I put up my hire sign and stopped the meter. I was just going to drive off when he put his hand up for me to stop, as if he'd changed his mind. He asked me where I was going, and I said I was going back to the office. He got in the cab again and told me to drop him at the Town Hall. That was on my way.'

'And you left him near the Town Hall ?'

'Yes, sir. I don't know which way he went from there. He stood at the kerb and watched me drive away.'

'And that's the truth ?'

'The whole truth, sir.'

'Why did you lie ?'

The dark eyes rolled to the manager, and away. 'From Chatham Street to the Town Hall I had my hire sign up. I forgot it. So the journey didn't register on the meter and I couldn't charge for it.'

'Be more careful another time,' said the manager sternly. 'We can't stay in business by giving free rides, but I'll overlook it this time because you told the truth about it.'

'Thank you, sir,' said Steelband humbly.

'Tell me,' said Martineau. 'When you had the man and the woman in the car, could you hear what they were talking about ?'

'No, sir. The dividing window was closed.'

'Could you *see* them talking, in the mirror ?'

'Yes, sir. They were talking.'

'Did they seem to be arguing or quarrelling ?'

'No, sir. They were talking serious and quiet.'

'Who did most of the talking ?'

'The gentleman at first, and then the girl.'

'Thank you. By the way, did you know that this was the police inspector who has been murdered ?'

'Yes, sir. I saw his picture in the paper. I was very sorry.'

'Why didn't you come forward and tell the police what you knew about him ?'

Again Steelband looked at the manager, then he said, 'I thought I was following general instructions. When I got this job I was told not to talk about fares, and what they did and where they went, so long as they behaved themselves. I was told if I kept my mouth shut I wouldn't get trouble.'

'Fair enough,' said the manager hastily, but heartily. 'Though next time one of your fares gets murdered, you can come and tell me, see ? Any more questions, Inspector?'

'Just a couple. Exactly where near the Town Hall did you drop Inspector McQuade, and what time ?'

'In the square right in front of the Town Hall, at about twenty-five minutes to nine.'

'Right, that will be all for the time being,' said Martineau.

'You've got nothing to worry about, Steelband,' said the manager.

The Jamaican turned away, palpably relieved. The policeman put away his pocket-book.

'I'll send a man to get a signed statement,' he said. 'Thanks very much for your help.'

'Any time, Inspector, any time,' said the manager, who believed in being on good terms with the police. 'Another cup of tea ?'

Martineau declined another cup of tea. Well satisfied with the result of his inquiry, he walked out of the taxi office. He had covered a little more of McQuade's time, and learned a little more about his movements, on the evening of the murder. McQuade had been alive, standing in front of the Town Hall and consequently only three minutes' walk from Police Headquarters, at twenty-five minutes to nine. Where had he gone from there?

Martineau strolled on meditatively. Though he was at the very hub of a thickly populated area, he saw few pedestrians and fewer vehicles. It was Sunday, and moreover it was teatime. On his route to Headquarters he came to Town Hall Square, and there he went out of his way a little. He crossed the square, and stood on the wide sidewalk in front of the Town Hall. He stood where Mick McQuade had stood six days ago, an hour or half an hour before his murder. He asked himself why McQuade had come to this particular spot. Had he wanted to call at Headquarters for something? Had he entered and left that place unnoticed?

Standing there, Martineau thought again about McQuade's movements on the day of his death. Mentally he followed the dead man's footsteps. The man had obviously been engaged on a private affair, the matter of his daughter's welfare. Until he had seen a man in a car; somebody he knew, or thought he knew. That, Martineau guessed, was when McQuade ceased to think about his daughter and once more became a policeman pure and simple : a policeman fairly pure and not so simple.

The unknown man had stopped his car by No. 5 Chatham Street. He had entered No. 5, or No. 3, or No. 7. McQuade had thought about staying on watch near those houses. He had paid off his taxi. Then he had changed his mind and ridden in the taxi to Town Hall Square. Why had he changed his mind, when some man he wanted was there, almost in his hands? It was only a matter of waiting for the man to come out to his car. And if anything went wrong, he still had the number of the car.

Martineau caught his breath. He stood perfectly still. That was it, the number of the car! Why hadn't he thought of that immediately. McQuade might not have been quite sure of a man only glimpsed in a passing car. He might also have wondered if the man lived at No. 3, 5, or 7 Chatham Street. He did not want to wait for hours, possibly many hours, for a man who might not be the man he wanted after all. So he had gone to the Town Hall.

Martineau turned, and looked at the main entrance of the great, black, Gothic building. He walked to it, and mounted the steps. The big double-leaf oaken door was locked. He rang the bell. There was always a porter on duty at the Town Hall.

In a little while there were stirrings at the other side of the door. A bolt shot back, and half of the door opened. Eyes behind thick glasses peered at the detective. 'What do you want ?' came the question.

'Police,' said Martineau. He brought out his warrant card, and opened it and held it in view. The porter stooped, and at a distance of two inches he read the name upon it.

'Martineau !' he said in surprise. He came upright, and peered with head back. 'Come in,' he said, opening the door wider. 'Happen you'll be wanting the licensing department, eh ?'

'Not at the moment,' said Martineau, stepping inside. 'Actually I'm wanting to know who was the porter on duty here between eight and nine last Monday night.'

The pebble glasses flashed as the head went back. 'Last Monday ? That 'ud be me and Joe Hatch. We were on nights last week. Change over today, see ? Joe ! Here a minute !'

From the snug porters' room came a round little man with a round, red, jolly face. He was in his early forties, and that made him a good twenty years younger than his colleague.

'Inspector Martineau,' said the older man, with just a touch of self-importance. 'He wants to know if we was on duty last Monday night.'

'Well, we was,' said Joe. And then he said, 'How dee do, sir.'

'How d'you do.' said Martineau. 'I want to know if you had a caller that night, between half-past eight and nine o'clock.'

'At that time I'd be going round the building,' said Joe. 'Old Tom here 'ud be on the door.'

The thick glasses flashed. 'I remember now,' said Tom. 'A man from the police came to look at motor licences. It happens so oft you're apt to forget.'

'You'll have to excuse Tom,' said Joe. 'He's on his last few months for his pension. We all have to help him, like. He can't see so well, nor remember neither.'

'This man from the police station, was he in uniform ?' Martineau asked.

'No, he were a detective same as you. He showed me his card, same as you did.'

'Did you read the name on the card ?'

'Aye, but I can't just remember it. Mac summat. I think there were a K in it.'

'Could your K have been a Q ?'

'Aye, happen it could, though I'm none so certain.'

Martineau brought out McQuade's photograph. 'Take a look at that,' he invited.

Tom held the picture to his nose. He peered at it for quite some time. 'It's like him. It could be him,' he said at last. 'But I wouldn't go on oath. It were dark then. Artificial light. I'm damn near blind in artificial light.'

Martineau nodded. He was reasonable sure that the caller had been McQuade. He would be quite sure after he had made inquiries to ascertain whether or not any other member of the C.I.D. had gone into the licensing department last Monday night.'

'Will you take me down there, and show me what he did ?' he asked.

'Course I will,' said Tom. 'I'll just get me keys.'

'I've got mine,' said Joe. 'I'll go with you.'

They went to the licensing department by an interior

route, which was a different matter from walking into it from the street. When Joe stopped at the inner door of the department, Martineau thought that they must have walked along half a mile of corridors.

'Let Tom lead the way now,' he said. 'It might help him to remember.'

Tom made his way into the record room of the department. It was like a corner of a public library. Thin files by the thousand were stacked on the shelves, and the rows of shelves marched in column down the narrow room. When the old man stopped uncertainly, halfway down the room, Martineau realized that he had no hope of getting any specific information from the record room. 'About here somewhere,' Tom said vaguely.

'Did it take him long to get what he wanted ?'

'Not two minutes,' said Tom eagerly, glad to be sure about something. 'He went to a shelf, happen about so high, and just sort of run his fingers along the files. He took one out and opened it. Then he wrote in his book and put the file back. That were all.'

'Thank you,' said Martineau. 'You've been a big help.' And he thought wryly that it was no wonder the murderer had taken McQuade's official pocket-book. His name and address were in it.

The two porters took him back to the main entrance and let him out. He went down the steps and stood before the Town Hall once more, and he reflected that it had been dark when McQuade came down these steps at about ten minutes to nine six days ago. It had been dark enough for murder. From there dear old Mick had gone straight to his death. The time limit did not allow for any other possibility.

Martineau had to cross the square to get to Head-quarters. Deep in thought, he walked to the pedestrian crossing. A car, dark-coloured, ordinary, unnoticeable— Austin, Morris, Ford, Standard, one of those—had just begun to move from the kerb a short distance away. In no hurry, Martineau stood at the kerb by the crossing and waited for the car to pass. But the car stopped and the driver signalled for him to cross. Such courtesy was by no means uncommon in Granchester. Martineau accepted it without a second thought. He did not even notice the face behind the windscreen of the car.

He stepped on to the crossing, and then the car leaped at him like a feral animal. He also leaped, in the direction he was going. That was nearly a fatal mistake. A second car, which he had not seen at all, was overtaking at speed. The driver of it neither swerved nor braked but steered straight for Martineau. The detective's brain and body worked with what—later—seemed to be miraculous quickness. Had he continued to go forward the driver of the second car would have caught him without difficulty. Some thought of that crossed his mind while he pirouetted like a dancer, though not so gracefully. A split-second's discrepancy in the murderous timing of the two cars allowed him to turn back. He jumped for car Number One as it went by, with no thought in mind but to get away from the faster vehicle. There was no running board. His arms were stretched ahead of him, and his big hands came down with a slap on the top of the car. There was nothing to grip. The driver reacted nervously to what might have appeared to be an attempt to board the car. He made a quick, slight swerve to the near side, and the car shrugged Martineau off. The edge of the rear wing caught his leg and destroyed his balance entirely. Briefly he was in the air, with car Number Two swerving in towards him. But Number Two's angle of approach was now too acute, and its speed was too great. Number Two could not hit Martineau without being involved in a crippling crash with Number One. The two cars sped on. The intended victim, arms still outstretched, landed face down with a breath-stealing thud in the road.

Gasping, he rolled over and sat up. The cars were now too far away for him to read number plates. And anyway he was in no condition to read number plates. And they were probably false numbers, or else the cars had been illegally borrowed for the purpose of killing him.

He was surprised to find that his boarding action and consequent aerial evolutions had taken him fully ten yards from the crossing. Then he looked down at his legs, and swore roundly. The trousers of his new suit were torn, and he could see blood. He wriggled his toes inside his shoe ; he moved his foot ; he examined the leg. There were abrasions and a long cut, but apparently no fracture. He rose painfully and limped to the kerb.

Two people came running across the square. They were a youth and a girl. The girl asked him if he was hurt, the youth went and picked up his hat.

'Do you want the ambulance, or anything ?' the boy asked as he proffered the hat. 'Heck, that was a near thing. And neither of 'em had the decency to stop. The cheeky beggars. On a crossing an' all.'

Martineau thanked him, and said that he did not need an ambulance. Apart from a few bruises, the cut leg was his only injury. He realized that he had been extremely fortunate. He had also been very careless. He perceived that he must give his secret enemy no chance to be third time lucky. Until Bashful was safely under lock and key Martineau would have to be on his guard all the time.

13

FROM TOWN HALL SQUARE Martineau made his way to Headquarters. In the C.I.D. lobby he met Chief Superintendent Clay, just going home for the day. Clay looked at his dusty clothes, torn trousers, and bleeding leg, and immediately ordered a car. 'Hospital for you, my lad, to get that leg stitched,' he said. 'I'll wait till you come back.'

An hour later, with his leg dressed and stitched, and wearing a pair of uniform trousers out of store, Martineau told the superintendent about his "accident."

The older man listened seriously. 'You've been damned lucky,' he said. 'Somebody is absolutely determined to get you off the strength one way or another. Twice in twenty-four hours is good going.'

'How on earth has Bashful managed to organize this second do, so soon after last night ?'

'He hasn't, in my opinion. Today's attempt was organized yesterday or the day before. Those fellows may have been stalking you all day, lying in wait and watching for their chance. Last night's effort was a brainwave, and it was done more or less on the spur of the moment by Bashful himself. He knew where you lived, he had the spray equipment, and he had the petrol. It's a pity you didn't see somebody's face today.'

'I hadn't time to look at faces. But if I'd done so we wouldn't have been any nearer to the main man. He recruits his help by letter and telephone as he did with Leon Crow and Bert Preston. Nobody is allowed to see him.'

'No, he's bashful all right. It makes you think that Leon Crow's death was no accident. What else have you been doing today, besides hopping about on pedestrian crossings ?'

Martineau told him. He nodded in a pleased way. 'You've done quite well,' he said, and that was high praise from him. 'You've got McQuade at ten minutes to nine in front of the Town Hall. You're on the last lap.'

'I believe I am. But where he went from there, I haven't a clue.'

'No, but you have a link.'

'Oh sure. Lennie Leroy. She's the next on my list.'

'And how do you propose to set about Miss Leroy ?'

'I'd like to keep observations on her, but I don't think I have the time. Our man is getting desperate. The strain might be too much for him. He might suddenly lose his nerve and clear out of the country. I don't want him to do that. I'm yearning to make his acquaintance.'

'So ?'

'I'll get a search warrant and look round her flat, in the hope of finding something. Then I'll talk to her.'

'And if she don't talk ?'

'If she won't talk it'll be just too bad,' said Martineau. He rose. 'I suppose I'd better be getting on with it.'

'Well, be careful,' were Clay's parting words. 'Your shy friend will be just about ready to start throwing hand grenades.'

Martineau went into the C.I.D. Devery was waiting for him. In his office, he passed on his new information to the sergeant. 'So now we're going to see Lennie Leroy,' he concluded. 'I'm going to get a warrant. Meanwhile, you find a couple of men.'

Half-an-hour later he returned to the C.I.D. with the warrant in his pocket. Devery was waiting for him, with Detective Constables Cassidy and Cook. In a C.I.D. car, with Devery driving, the four men went to Chatham Street.

As Martineau looked up at the long terrace of converted houses he never thought of sending a man to the back door. He was thinking in terms of a search rather than a raid, and that was an attitude he was to regret. The car stopped at No. 5, and the four men got out, in plain view of anyone who might be looking from the windows above. Martineau led the way up the stairs to 5D. He pressed the bell button beside the door. He waited.

This time he heard no brisk click of heels approaching the door. A woman in her bare feet may walk with as little noise as a cat. Instead of the click of heels he heard the click of a dead latch, and nothing more. He tried the door. It would not open. It was then that he thought of a back door.

He whispered urgently to Cassidy and Cook. 'Get to the back door, quick. Stop anybody who comes out.'

Not realizing why Martineau had whispered his order, the two men went galloping noisily down the stairs. The inspector cursed under his breath. Devery wisely kept quiet.

Martineau rang the bell again, and then he pounded with his fists on the door. He knew from experience that the peremptory thunder of a policeman's knock may have its own psychological effect. He had known it compel people to open a door when they did not intend any such action.

He heard a woman's voice. 'Who's there?'

'Police,' he rasped. 'Open this door or I'll break it down.'

Lennie Leroy opened the door a little way. The inspector saw her eyes, and part of a flushed face. He was about to push the door open when she said, 'You'll have to wait a minute. I'm naked.'

That stopped him. 'Leave the door as it is and go and put something on,' he ordered. 'I'll give you exactly thirty seconds.'

141

She went away. He looked at the second hand on his watch. When it had ticked off half a minute he pushed open the door and strode through the narrow hallway to the living-room. Lennie Leroy was just emerging from the bedroom, knotting the belt of a dressing gown. Her feet were in high-heeled mules, which she certainly had not been wearing when she answered the door. Her remarkable red hair was in slight disarray, but still very becoming. Her face was still flushed.

'Keep an eye on her,' the inspector said to Devery. Then he made a quick tour of the flat. He did not find the man he hoped to find, but he found the back door where the man had escaped. He muttered maledictions, blaming himself. He had made a cardinal error. He had had his man almost in his hands and through lack of fore-sight he had let him escape. He was quite sure of this. One thing he had noticed as he strode into the living-room. A tray of drinks, and among other articles on the tray were a silver tankard, a champagne bottle, and a brandy bottle. The man who now eluded him was the man who had fled from W. S. Hope's office. This was the shy man who drank champagne laced with brandy, a millionaire's drink. Martineau now remembered the name of the concoction. It was called King's Peg.

The back door gave access to what had been the service stairs of the house, the stairs up which, in the glorious days of the nineteenth century, ten-year-old maids had toiled with buckets of coal to keep the quality warm. It was still the backstairs, but now it was a dodger's exit, like the backstairs of W. S. Hope's office.

Martineau went down the stairs and found the back door of the house. There was a large backyard, with a wide gate standing open. He went out into the back street. Cassidy was just outside the gate. Cook was not in sight.

'Where's your mate?' he demanded.

Cassidy pointed to the far end of the street. 'He'll be

coming round, sir. On the ground floor we couldn't get through to the back. There was a door, but it was locked. We ran out to the front and separated. I was fifty yards from my end of the block, Cook was about three-fifty from his end. He set off to run.'

'There was a car,' said Martineau.

'Sergeant Devery has the ignition key in his pocket, sir.'

Martineau nodded. Devery, responsible for the C.I.D. car, had naturally not left the key in the dashboard. Devery ought to have been sent down the stairs with Cassidy, instead of Cook. Another mistake. Martineau began to wonder if the incident in Town Hall Square had shaken his brain a little.

'I saw him, sir. Or at least I saw his car,' said Cassidy. 'He was away on the street, going like a bat outa hell, when I came round the corner there. A black car. That's all I can tell you about it.'

Martineau nodded again, and stared moodily at the distant figure of Cook, who had appeared at the far end of the back street. Cook came on at a jog trot.

'Well ?' said the inspector, when he arrived.

The plain clothes man shook his head. He was out of breath. 'Car,' he said. 'Too far ahead. Black. Rover I think. One person in it. Couldn't get number.'

'Did you get a good look at the driver ?'

'No, sir.'

So Miss Leroy's visitor had got clean away, and it was nobody's fault but Martineau's. That person sighed, but made no comment. In common with other police officers of any rank, he was not in the habit of drawing attention to his own mistakes.

He returned to the backyard of No. 5, and his men followed him. He looked round thoughtfully. The man whom Popsie had called Lennie Leroy's "rich bloke" was apparently in the habit of leaving his car in the yard when he called to spend an hour or two with his girl. But six days ago, when McQuade had seen the car, it had been left at the front of the house. Probably on that occasion the rich bloke had called to pick up Miss Leroy and take her out or, more probably, to leave a message. He had called to leave a message because the girl had no telephone. The girl had no telephone because, with the present congestion of Post Office lines, the only phone she would be able to get would be on a party line. A confirmed back-door visitor like her lover would want to have nothing to do with a party line.

He thought about the man, and about his expensive drinking habits. In his mind's eye he saw again the bottles and glasses on the tray. He presumed that Devery would have enough wit to prevent Leroy from moving those glasses and washing them. There was just a chance that they might hold a good finger-print.

But finger-prints would have to be taken without Leroy's knowledge. Above all, Martineau did not want to scare away the man he pursued. He wanted him to remain on his, Martineau's, "manor." *If* the unknown man had a police record, nothing would get him out of the district quicker than a message from his girl to the effect that the police had dusted the flat for finger-prints.

'We're going to pretend to search the girl's place,' he said to Cassidy. 'I want you to be careful not to leave any dabs, and to be careful not to spoil any which might be there.'

'Yessir,' said Cassidy.

'For you, Cook,' the inspector went on, 'I've got a different sort of job. Now listen carefully. The Leroy girl hasn't seen you yet, and she's not going to see you. You'll come with me up the backstairs of the flat, so that you'll know your way. But you won't enter. You'll go quietly downstairs again and find a phone, and you'll get in touch with Sergeant Bird.'

'I may not be able to reach him, sir. He's on Weekly Rest Day.'

'Get Bird if you can. If you can't, get one or two of his men. On my orders they're to come here, bringing all their tackle. You'll meet them and take them in the back way. You'll find the search warrant on the kitchen table. I want every identifiable finger-print in the place, understand ?'

'Yessir.'

'I want a good job and a quick job, and I don't want Bird or his men to leave any traces. When they've done, you'll see that the place is left secure. Is that clear ?'

'Yessir,' said Cook.

Martineau took the search warrant from his pocket and handed it to Cassidy. 'When we are about to leave for Headquarters with Miss Leroy,' he said, 'I shall tell you to go and make sure that the back door is locked. You'll make sure that it *isn't* locked, and you'll leave this warrant on the kitchen table. Is *that* clear ?'

'Yessir,' said Cassidy.

'All right,' said the inspector. 'Let's go.'

They entered the house and climbed the backstairs to the flat, then Cook returned to the street as directed. The other two went through the tiny kitchen to the living-room. Devery was standing rather self-consciously with his back to the fireplace. Miss Leroy sprawled carelessly in an easy chair, smoking a cigarette. She was still wearing nothing but a dressing gown, and she was showing quite a lot of bare leg and bosom. Now, her colour was normal. She stared disdainfully at Martineau and Cassidy as they entered.

A casual, guarded glance assured Martineau that the tray of drinks was still there, apparently untouched since he last saw it. He turned to the girl. 'You told me a lie about never having met Inspector McQuade,' he said directly.

She gazed at him defiantly. 'It was only because I didn't want to be mixed up in a murder case,' she said.

'Well, you are mixed up in one. I'm taking you to Headquarters for interrogation. Go and get some clothes on.'

She glared at the big policeman. There was a clash of wills. 'You can't make me,' she retorted sulkily.

'Go and get dressed,' he said with contempt.

She stood up. She flung her cigarette in the general direction of the fireplace. 'All right, you can wait,' she said with venom as she moved towards the bedroom. 'It's going to take me a long time to dress.'

Martineau grinned at her. 'That will give us plenty of time to look around,' he said. 'Is that bureau locked ?'

'You leave my letters alone !' she flared, and then the bedroom door closed behind her.

'All right, men,' said Martineau, not caring whether or not he could be heard in the other room. 'We'll have a *dekko* at the place. I don't think we shall find anything much.'

But then he made a furtive signal to Devery. He spread his hand over a polished table, nearly touching it. Then he withdrew his hand and shook his head. The sergeant nodded.

They did not have much time to search. With the knowledge that the police were handling her possessions, and perhaps surreptitiously drinking her liquor, Lennie Leroy dressed very quickly indeed. In a few minutes she reappeared, attired for the street.

'All right, you can sit down for a minute,' said Martineau. And to his henchmen, 'You two have a quick gander round the bedroom.'

The two men went into the bedroom. Martineau closed the bureau, having glanced at its contents and found nothing which appeared to have any connection with the

McQuade job. 'Here, have a cigarette,' he said, offering his packet of Players to the girl.

Rather to his surprise, she accepted a cigarette. No doubt it was a habit of hers to accept things from men. 'Some people have a nerve,' she said, referring to Martineau's inspection of the bureau's contents.

'My curiosity isn't personal, I assure you,' he said. 'I've got to get my facts any way I can.' He stooped and picked up an ashtray, holding it daintily with forefinger and thumb just touching the rim. He peered at cigarette butts. They looked like the remains of ordinary standard-size cigarettes. Some bore signs of lipstick, some did not. 'Tell me,' he said. 'What did Inspector McQuade want with you ?'

'Why should I tell you ?' she asked, but quietly.

'Is there any reason why you shouldn't ?'

'Sure. I don't like you.'

He smiled. 'Would you sooner tell it to some other policeman ?'

'All coppers are the same to me.'

'Suppose *I* tell *you* ? Do I get an honest Yes or No ?'

'That depends on whether I want to answer or not.'

'The longer you take to answer, the more I shall keep on asking you. I'm in no hurry. I've got all night and I'm not tired.'

'Oh, be damned to you,' she said impatiently. 'He told me about Barry Hill and his daughter. He thought I'd help him to stop it.'

'He assumed that you and Hill were—sweethearts ?'

'Something like that. He asked me if I'd confront Barry and the girl, and make with the jealousy. Accuse him of two-timing, and all that.'

'And did you agree ?'

'I did, sort of. I—well, Barry had just given me the polite brush-off, and I was mad. When I knew he'd turn me down for a bloody copper's daughter, I was madder still. Then I suddenly realized that somebody else might get mad, too. It struck me that Barry might carve me up if I ruined his romance. I told the inspector so.'

'And what did he say to that ?'

'He said he'd guarantee that Barry wouldn't lay a finger on me. But I don't go much on coppers' promises.'

Martineau regarded the girl shrewdly. 'So then he offered you money,' he guessed.

'Yes,' she admitted. 'He started with a tenner, and went up to fifty. It was worth that much to him.'

'I imagine that his daughter's future happiness was worth a good deal more than that to him. So you turned him down ?'

'I did, more or less. But the taxi was at my door then, and he said he'd leave me to think it over. He said he'd get in touch with me again quite soon.'

'And then ?'

'Then I got out of the taxi, and he drove off in it. I came indoors.'

'And then you had a caller,' said Martineau, but he said it to himself. He had no intention of letting this girl know that there was any other link between McQuade and herself. Not yet, at any rate.

He studied the girl, and the fact that she was handsome enough to be well worth studying did not cross his mind. But something else did.

'Apart from Hill's possible violence,' he asked, 'was there any other reason why you were afraid to make him your enemy ?'

'No,' she said. 'Oh, no !'

He did not believe her, but for the time being he pretended that he did.

'By the way,' he asked curiously, as if the answer to the question could not be of the slightest importance to him, 'who was the chap who skeddaddled out of here when I came to the front door ?'

'What chap?' she retorted. 'There was nobody here but me. I'd just been having a bath when you came.'

Martineau did not let his glance shift to the tray of drinks. If the girl chose to delude herself that he had not noticed it, that was all to the good.

Devery and Cassidy emerged from the bedroom.

'Nothing in there, sir,' said the sergeant.

'All right,' said Martineau. 'We'll all take a little ride to Headquarters. Oh, Cassidy. Just go and make sure that the back door is secure, will you?'

14

AT HEADQUARTERS, Martineau found that he and Lennie Leroy had time on their hands. He did not want to arouse her suspicion by questioning her too persistently about the man who had got away, and she seemed to have told him as much as she knew about Inspector McQuade. He talked to her for a few minutes about Barry Hill, and found her reticent in respect of her relations with him. To pass the time he took a statement from her in longhand, questioning her about each point and then putting it down as carefully as if he were writing in the charge book. He brought great solemnity to the task, and without doubt the girl thought that it was for the sole purpose of giving a statement that she had been brought to the police station.

When the statement was completed, and, after a small argument, signed, he murmured something vague about "checking up," and left Miss Leroy in the care of Devery and Cassidy. He went into the main C.I.D. office, saw the detective inspector on duty, and arranged for observations to be kept upon the girl. He insisted that the shadowing must cover twenty-four hours of the day, twenty-four hours of every day until he had discovered the identity and whereabouts of the "rich bloke."

While he discussed the matter with the inspector, he looked anxiously through the window at the sky. The time was eight o'clock, and the light was fading. Sergeant Bird's flash-bulbs would be making sheet lightning effects inside Lennie Leroy's flat. He hoped that the flashing lights would not make any of her neighbours curious enough to question her.

Then Cook entered the office, with the search warrant in his hand. 'Did Bird find anything ?' was Martineau's eager question as he took the warrant.

'He seemed to find plenty, sir,' Cook replied. 'One complete set of the right hand on the bedroom window was a beauty. From the span it looks like a man's print. There's a dressing-table in front of the window. Somebody leaned over it to look down into the street, and steadied himself by putting his finger-tips on the window.'

'Good. And is all clear ?'

'All clear and all secure, sir. And everything just as it was.'

'Fine, fine.' Martineau went so far as to slap the plain clothes man on the shoulder. He went to his own office.

'How much longer am I going to be kept here ?' Leroy demanded.

'You are at liberty to go, with my thanks for the statement you have given,' said the inspector genially. 'A car will take you home, or anywhere you want to go within reason.'

'I'm not going home,' she said, with a very faint answering smile. 'The car had better take me to the Northland Hotel.'

'See to it, Cassidy,' said Martineau, and the girl departed with the big Irishman.

When she had gone, the inspector went to Sergeant Bird's department. Devery went to one of the soundproof telephone booths in the C.I.D. office. These were designed for the reception and delivery of confidential information, and they were not extensions of the police switchboard. He dialled the number of the Northland Hotel, and asked if he could speak briefly with Ella Bowie. In idle moments that attractive woman had been on his mind, and now he had an excuse to speak to her.

151

She came on the line. He asked her how she was. She said she was lonely.

'With all those admiring fellows propping up the bar ?' Devery queried. 'You can't be.'

'I'm lonely in a crowd,' she retorted. 'Why don't you come on over ? If you can get rid of that boss of yours.'

'Well, I'm not at liberty right now,' he hedged.

'Well then, later. We close at ten on Sundays, you know.'

He knew what she meant. That he should take her home. She lived alone. She loved him and she wanted him. He was strongly attracted to her, but he had a feeling that a close association with her would eventually lead to trouble for him. That was one of the reasons why he had avoided her. Well, he thought, we only live once.

'I'll be around before ten,' he said. '*If* I can get away.'

'Oh, darling !' It was an exclamation of consummate happiness.

'In the meantime,' he went on, 'I want you to do something for me. Do you know a woman called Lennie Leroy ?'

'I do. She comes in here sometimes.'

'She's on her way now, I believe. Just keep an eye on her for me, will you ? Remember who she talks to, and all that.'

'I'll do that, darling. Now I must get back to the bar. See you later,' she babbled joyfully, and then she was gone.

In the meantime, Martineau had walked into Sergeant Bird's office. Bird was the Force's specialist in finger-prints, palm-prints, etc., and photography. It was generally believed in the Force that Sergeant Bird was getting his time in very nicely, with hours of ease out of sight and sound of other policemen, but now he was very busy indeed. Already he had his coat off and his sleeves rolled up. He was bending over a long table, carefully arranging numbered labels, each label describing the exact place in Lennie Leroy's flat where finger-prints had been found.

'Good evening, sir,' he said when he saw Martineau. 'My wife is going to shoot you when she sees you.'

The inspector grinned. 'Sorry I ruined your day off,' he said. 'However, Mrs. Bird can admire the medal when you get it.'

'Important as all that, is it ? Have we got our murderer here ?'

'There's just a chance. How long will you be with this lot ?'

'Hours,' said Bird. 'Hours and bloody hours.'

'I shall want you on the job by nine o'clock in the morning. You'll have to send off your forms as usual to the Yard.'

'I'll do that tonight, before I go home. Wakefield as well.'

'You won't send anything to Wakefield.'

Bird straightened his back. He stared at Martineau. It was customary to send all finger-print inquiries to both New Scotland Yard and Wakefield, the two great clearing houses of crime in England. 'Why not, sir ?' he asked.

'Wakefield can't be much more than forty miles from here. You'll take a car and go there in the morning. That'll be quicker than waiting for the post. And if you find anything good I want you to phone the news from Wakefield, instead of waiting to tell me when you get back. That way, you won't be tempted to break your neck on the return journey.'

'Very good, sir. I'll do that.'

'Be sure there's no mistake. It may be of the greatest importance.'

'There will be no mistake, sir.'

'Right. Good night,' said Martineau.

He returned to the C.I.D., where Devery was waiting for him. 'We'll call it a day,' he said. 'And what a day it's been. A long, hard day.'

Devery grinned sympathetically. 'Dawn to dusk for you, sir,' he said. 'You must be dog tired.'

'I am. And tonight, no doubt, I shall be sleeping on the sofa at my mother-in-law's house. I must get there and see how Julia and the child are getting on.'

'I'd have a car and a driver if I were you. It's getting dark, and you're weary. You can't stand another attempt to get you off the strength.'

'Thank you for that suggestion, laddie. I'll have a car. And on the way home I'll call and see what's left of my house.'

'I'll come with you, sir, if I may. I can ride back in the car.'

'Look here, young fellow-me-lad. It hasn't come to the point where I need an escort.'

'It isn't that. I have nothing to do for an hour or so.'

'All right,' Martineau growled. 'Come if you like.' He rang for a car.

Though tired, he was in good spirits, and in the car he talked optimistically about the possibilities of the morrow. But the sight of his house depressed him. What had been a snug home was now a roofless ruin. There was a small crowd staring at it, and a policeman on guard, though it was hard to imagine what there could have been to tempt looters. He prowled disconsolately among the ashes and rubble, and gazed sadly at the few fragments of twisted metal which were the remains of his beloved piano. Then he went next door, to the other house of the semi-detached pair. It had not been greatly damaged, but he sympathized with his neighbour, and received sympathy. 'I shan't live there again,' he said to Devery when they had returned to the car. 'Whatever the insurance people decide, I'll get rid of it. Thank God, it was paid for.'

At the home of his mother-in-law, which was another small semi-detached house similar to his own, he found his child asleep in bed and his wife sitting quite comfortably by the fireside. He reflected ruefully that she could

154

settle at *that* fireside all right, just as if she had never left it. And then he thought, "It's as well she can."

Devery looked in to pay his respects to Mrs. Martineau, then he returned to the car. As it moved away from the house he noticed a loitering figure. It was a man he knew, a plain clothes man attached to that suburban division. Apparently Superintendent Clay was doing his best to safeguard Martineau and his family until Bashful had been laid by the heels.

Devery asked the driver to drop him at the junction of Bishopsgate and Lacy Street, and from there he sauntered to the Northland Hotel. He had to compel himself to saunter. He wanted to walk fast. The attraction of Ella pulled him like a magnet. His heart was beating quickly. He was excited even before he met her.

She was looking for him. She saw him as soon as he appeared in the doorway of her bar. And yet, such is the way of women, she appeared to be perfectly composed. The hungry look had gone. He had entered that bar to see her and no one else. She was content.

She served him with half-a-pint of beer. 'Back in a moment,' she said, because other customers were waiting to be served. He was happy to drink his beer and look at her. He loved the way she moved. Her own happiness put gaiety into her every action, but, he reflected, there was more to it than that. She moved like the *premiere danseuse* of a ballet called *Woman*.

When she returned to him she said, prosaically enough, 'The lady you were asking about came and went. Seemingly there was nobody here she wanted to talk to. She had one drink and she had to buy it herself. So she buzzed off.'

'Didn't she talk to anybody at all ?'

'Only me, when she ordered a drink. We don't like each other, so you could hardly call that talking.'

Devery grinned. 'She despises you because you work

for a living ; you despise her because she doesn't. Is that
it ?'

'Something like that. I believe she's a kept woman,
though I don't know who keeps her.'

"I wish you did," said Devery to himself.

'In case you're interested,' she went on, 'the swell
mobster is still hand-in-glove with his new woman. Something going on there, I wouldn't be surprised.'

He noticed that once more she refrained from uttering
Dixie Costello's name. Many people were like that, he
reflected. They were afraid. Well, this girl had reason to
be afraid. She had been razor-slashed once. Not at Dixie's
orders, but by one of his men. Aloud he said, 'What do
you mean, something going on ? Do you mean—loverlike ?'

She flashed him a cheeky smile and rolled her eyes.
'That's what I do mean. That's the bait she's using on
him, unless my eyes deceive me. She wants something
from him, though goodness knows what it can be. She's
'way above his class. It'll tickle him to death to take the
pants off a propah loidy.'

Women, he thought. Ella was talking like that with the
deliberate intention of bringing erotic images to his mind.
She was determined that he should not escape her that
night.

She moved away to serve some customers. He watched
her. Desire stirred in him. The thing was on again. He
knew her. She would take him home with her, and then ...
It was not so much that she would deny him nothing, but
that she would demand everything from him. He would
be in the toils, and liking it.

As an afterthought, he hoped that she would have
something in for supper. He had nothing to eat since early
afternoon.

. . . . .

Monday was yet another mild, sunny day, and early-
risen housewives were already hanging out newly-washed

clothes when Martineau went to work. His leg was sore, but he was rested. He had not been compelled to sleep on the sofa at his mother-in-law's house. That lady had provided a comfortable bed for himself and Julia.

He limped into Headquarters at nine o'clock and, as usual, he found the ambitious Devery waiting for him. Devery was spruce and well-shaved as ever, and, Martineau thought, he looked as fit as a flea.

'There's nothing much on the agenda until we hear from Sergeant Bird,' the inspector said. 'We just have to see those two characters Drax and Taylor, and they won't be at work yet. If one of those two keeps on making himself hard to find I'll start thinking he might be our man.'

'Not in Scotland or London at all,' said Devery, 'but being a bad lad in Granchester.'

'That could be. Anyway, we won't phone for appointments. We'll barge in, whether we're welcome or not.'

Neither of them felt like doing any paper work, though it would have to be done sooner or later. They sat in Martineau's office and smoked and talked. Then they went out for coffee. They passed on more than an hour that way. Then Martineau looked at his watch.

'Bird will be steaming into Wakefield any time now,' he said. 'And it's time we got busy. We'll go and see if we can get a glimpse of Mr. Eugene Drax.'

The offices of Drax and Weaver were in the tight little financial district between Town Hall Square and Lacy Street, and they were some ten minutes' walk from Headquarters. And in the same district were the offices of William Taylor. Nevertheless, Devery suggested the use of a car.

'Nonsense,' said Martineau. 'I don't want this leg of mine to stiffen up entirely. It's a grand morning and we have plenty of time. We'll walk.'

They walked, and if Martineau was not on the alert, Devery certainly was. But he saw nothing to make him suspicious, and their progress was interrupted by nothing more than the normal delays caused by traffic.

The Drax-Weaver suite appeared to consist of three rooms. A large outer room, with chairs for callers and desks for two typists, two junior accountants, and an elderly clerk, and two inner rooms named respectively Drax and Weaver. When the two policemen walked into the outer room one of the typists looked up with a bright smile. Apparently she was also the receptionist.

'Good morning,' she said.

'Good morning. I am Chief Inspector Martineau of the City Police. I would like to see Mr. Drax.'

The inevitable question came. 'Have you an appointment ?'

'No. But would you tell Mr. Drax that I won't interrupt his work for more than a couple of minutes.'

The girl looked doubtful. 'Take a seat, will you ?' she invited. She entered the office marked Drax, and closed the door behind her. Half a minute later she returned.

'I'm sorry,' she said. 'Mr. Drax is terribly busy. He had to come back from Scotland yesterday specially to attend to some urgent business this morning. He can't see you today.'

Martineau smiled. 'Thank you,' he said. He rose, then he walked to Drax's room and entered. Devery followed him. Protesting, the girl followed Devery.

A small, elderly man sat at the desk in the room. He had silvery hair, a baby-pink complexion, flinty eyes and tight lips. He was so small that he did not look strong enough to pull a salmon out of the Tweed.

'Are you Eugene Drax ?' Martineau asked.

The man looked up from his work. He was quite composed. 'I am,' he said. 'And this is my office. What is the meaning of this intrusion ?'

'I wanted to see if you were the man I'm looking for.'

'And am I ?'

158

'No.'

'Good.' The man's thin-lipped smile curled at the corners of his mouth. 'I suppose you are this man Martineau. You will be interested to learn that I shall report your act of bullying trespass to the Chief Constable.'

Martineau was unimpressed. 'You'll get no satisfaction from it. You'll get an acknowledgment, that's all. Whether or not the Chief Constable acts upon your complaint, you'll never know.'

'I will, if he compels you to come here and apologize to me.'

Martineau's face showed surprise. 'Oh, an apology,' he said largely. 'Is that all you want ? I apologize. I apologize for entering this room. I also apologize to the young lady here. And so does my sergeant. And now good day.'

Eugene Drax no longer smiled. His face had turned a deeper pink. 'Good day, and be damned to you,' he snapped.

Martineau walked out smiling, but when he and Devery were off the premises he said, 'Coo, don't you meet some sons of unsuccessful prostitutes on this job ?'

They went round to William Taylor's place, and there they had a different reception. True, the girl wanted to know if they had an appointment. She went to an inner office to see Mr. Taylor. But when she returned she said that Mr. Taylor was engaged on the telephone, and would see them in a few minutes if they cared to wait.

They cared to wait, and while they waited Martineau reflected that William Taylor was the last man on his list of people involved in the Bassey case. What a waste of time the Bassey affair had been to him, he thought. Mick McQuade had been engaged upon a different matter entirely when he had encountered the man who killed him : the same man, presumably, who was now trying to kill the only other policeman who knew him. This business of seeing Drax and Taylor was a farce. It was just a matter of completing the list, of leaving no loose ends, of being in a position to affirm that no possibility had been over-looked.

With regard to the last man, Taylor, Martineau re-membered an item of information which he had seen on McQuade's file of the Bassey case. Somehow McQuade had learned that Taylor was a director of Granchester Textiles, and he had seen fit to make a note of it. Just one of those things, Martineau supposed. McQuade was a man who would store up every scrap of information, in the hope that it might click into line with other information.

Then they went in to see Taylor. Like Eugene Drax, he was small and elderly. Unlike Drax, he was benign. Much too benign to be a successful financier, Martineau thought at first. And then he remembered that many successful men were good men, and on the average more benevolent than the unsuccessful ones, because they could afford to be.

He discovered that he knew Taylor by sight. He would not have mentioned this, but Taylor also knew him. 'So *you* are Chief Inspector Martineau,' the financier said, coming forward to shake hands. 'You were once a Good Samaritan to me. The winter before last. Do you re-member ?'

Martineau smiled and said that he did remember. He also said that it was a small enough thing to be forgotten. One morning Taylor had fallen in a frozen rut in a narrow snowbound street near the Stock Exchange. Martineau had come upon him and found that he had a broken ankle. Since no vehicle except a snowplough could get to him, the inspector had picked him up and carried him to the nearest main road. Taylor had insisted that he did not want an ambulance, so Martineau had put him in a taxi.

'Was it a fracture, sir ?' he asked.

'It was indeed, and it is still a confounded nuisance. But for your kindness I might have had to lie there until I got my death of cold.'

In daylight, in the heart of Granchester, that would have been extremely unlikely. Smiling, Martineau shook his head.

'Well, never mind,' said Taylor. 'The thing is that we meet again.' He looked at his watch. 'I don't think it's too early for us to have a drink, do you ?'

In those circumstances it would have been churlish to refuse. Martineau did not usually make any bones about being churlish, but he found himself liking William Taylor. Also, an idea was forming in his mind that the man might be useful to him.

'It's just the morning for a nice long drink,' he said.

Taylor opened a cupboard in his desk. 'I haven't beer, I'm afraid,' he said. 'Let's see. Here's a very fair dry sherry. Not too dry, mind you. Then there's whisky, gin, vermouth. Oh, and there's a bottle of brandy. Didn't know I had that.'

Martineau and Devery settled for tall whiskies-and-soda, and Taylor decided that he would have the same. He poured generously, and then had to be encouraged with the soda. He handed over the drinks ceremoniously. 'Your very good health, gentlemen,' he said.

They responded, and then after a suitable brief silence in appreciation of the liquor, Martineau remarked : 'Speaking of brandy, Mr. Taylor, have you ever tried a King's Peg ?'

Taylor frowned in thought. 'King's Peg ? Isn't that brandy topped up with champagne ?'

'That's more-or-less what it is.'

'No, I've never had it. I did know a fellow who used to drink it, though. Now then, what the deuce was his name ?'

Inwardly tense, the two policemen sat with looks of polite interest on their faces.

'Hare, was it ?' Mr. Taylor asked himself. 'Haines ? Harmer ? Some such name. I can't remember. Anyway, he found he couldn't afford the champagne—so he said—

and he started taking his brandy straight. He died of the brandy.'

Martineau and Devery relaxed. Taylor went on, 'I don't suppose you fellows have come here on a purely social visit. What can I do for you ?'

When he had entered the office, Martineau had only wanted to set eyes upon William Taylor and then depart. Now, he had time to spare and he thought he could learn something. He was wondering just how he would have got his information if he had started an inquiry about Granchester Textile shares on behalf of Sylvia Paris. Also, now that Mrs. Paris was teamed up with Dixie Costello anything could happen. The information itself might be useful.

'I have come to you for advice, Mr. Taylor,' he said. 'My police experience has never taken me into the realm of stocks and shares, and now I'm like a lost child crying in the wilderness.'

Taylor smiled indulgently. 'What is this terrible problem, Chief Inspector ?'

'Well, first of all I want to impress upon you that this business is absolutely confidential, even if it never comes to anything.'

Taylor nodded gravely. 'I understand how a police inquiry may well be confidential. I won't say a word about it to a soul. On my honour.'

'Thank you,' said Martineau. 'You see, sir, there's been an allegation of sharp practice. Without going to the trouble of getting a court order, where could a policeman get to know about the disposition of a company's shares ?'

'At Bush House, in London. You can get the share position after the end of each financial year.'

'I may want to work on closer dates than those.'

'Ah. Any particular shares ?'

'Granchester Textiles.'

Taylor sat up straight. 'Oh dear,' he said. 'I don't know if you ought to go on. It may be a matter about which

I cannot remain silent. You see, I am on the board of G.T.'

'I know. And I'll take a chance on your being able to remain silent.'

'Did you come to me because you knew I was a director ?'

'No. I came to see if a man calling himself William Taylor was a certain man I wanted. While I was waiting out there I recalled that you were a director of G.T. Do you remember the big fire about a year ago ?'

'I certainly do.'

'How would it be possible for me to get to know exactly who bought and sold G.T. shares before and after the fire ? Is there anybody who would know ?'

'Yes. The registrar would know.'

'Registrar ?'

'Nearly all big companies employ a man to keep a register of all transactions in which the company's shares are involved.'

'Would the registrar pass on any of that information to the police ?'

'I don't think he would. At least not without explicit permission from the board.'

'But would he give it to a director ?'

'Without hesitation. Or to any shareholder on payment of a shilling.'

Said Martineau bluntly, 'I'd be grateful if some director would get it for me.'

Taylor smiled. 'That director being myself, of course. Before I did anything like that, I would want to know more about the case. For instance, would any subsequent police action result in damaging publicity for G.T. ?'

'I don't see how it could. The firm can't be blamed for the actions of individual shareholders.'

'What is the story ?'

'It's an unsupported allegation, by a woman. And even if she is correct in what she says, the thing may not amount

163

to an indictable crime. But she's trying to bring another person into the business, and this person I don't trust at all. There's no telling what he might do, or how the thing might develop. I want to be one jump ahead of him. A policeman's job is the prevention and detection of crime. Prevention comes first.'

'That is the part of your work that doesn't get into the papers.'

'That is so, Mr. Taylor. Now this is the story, true or otherwise. Sylvia Paris, a widow, had a big block of G.T. shares left by her husband. A man called Lionel Hart wanted those shares, as cheap as he could get them I suppose. The morning after the big fire he put all his own shares on the market. If he had any associates I suppose they would do the same. Then he phoned Mrs. Paris and told her that he had some inside information. He said that G.T. had been stocking inflammable material in a warehouse or part of a warehouse which wasn't covered by insurance for the stocking of this particular material. He said that the insurance people had discovered this, and that they were not going to pay the claim, which would be something in the region of a million pounds. A million pounds loss is a big blow to any company. Hart advised Mrs. Paris to get rid of her shares immediately. He had been in the habit of giving her stock market tips, and she thought that this was just another one. She unloaded her shares.'

'Hart may have told his story to other people as well,' said Taylor. 'Quite a lot of G.T. shares were on the market that morning. There may even have been a mild panic. Anyway, the shares dropped in price for a short time.'

'For a very short time. Someone bought them in. Mrs. Paris thinks that it was Lionel Hart who bought them, getting as many as he could at a very nice price.'

'Well,' said Taylor. 'If it's true, it was a damnable trick to play on a widow woman, rich or poor. I'll find out who sold and bought G.T. shares about the time of the fire, and I'll let you know. I'll do it today.'

'Thank you,' said Martineau.

'Is that all you want ?'

'That is all, sir. If Sergeant Devery comes here about five o'clock this afternoon, will you have the information for him ?'

'Yes. And now will you have another drink ?'

'I don't mind if I do, sir. Just the one. I think I'm going to have a strenuous day. I may as well relax in good company while I have the chance.'

Mr. Taylor refilled glasses, and passed them over as ceremoniously as before. He raised his own glass.

'Confusion to your enemies,' he said.

15

DETECTIVE SERGEANT BIRD was proudly aware of the importance of finger-prints in police work. He was also proud in his belief that he knew as much about them as anybody. Why, he would tell you, he had lectured on finger-prints. Mind you, he would readily admit that the finding of a clear finger-print of a criminal on the scene of a major crime was a rare occurrence in modern times, but as readily he would point out that the solving of crimes was not the main use of finger-prints. The main use of "dabs," he would let you know, was for the sure identification of persons already in custody, so that they could not hide their long, bad records behind false names. In many vocations, he would say, a man who had had ill luck might make a fresh start by going elsewhere and changing his name. But not in crime. There were no successful fresh starts in crime, because after the first arrest under a new name the police would unearth the old one.

But the finger-prints found in Lennie Leroy's flat provided Sergeant Bird with a new experience. Never before had he had an inquiry so urgent that he had had to travel with the forms himself, and never had he handled an inquiry of quite this nature. So far as he knew there had been no crime committed in the flat, and there was no person in custody to be identified. This was a matter of find the real name of a mystery man whom none of his colleagues had yet seen clearly. This was something special.

At the West Riding Police Headquarters in Wakefield,

at eleven o'clock in the forenoon of that Monday in April, Bird found a name he had never expected to find. His heart beat fast when he saw it. He made sure of it, satisfying himself as to loops, whorls, arches and individual characteristics so that he would have gone on oath at the assizes about it.

'I thought so,' he said with forced calm, to the young West Riding man who was assisting him. 'No, I don't need to see his record. We have that in Granchester, but not his prints.'

'One of yours, is he ?' asked the Riding man, who was too young a policeman to know the significance of the name he had just read.

'He soon will be, I hope.'

'You're not on that McQuade murder job, are you ?' came the shrewd question.

'God bless us, no,' the sergeant lied boldly. He didn't much like to deceive a fellow officer who had been most obliging, but he had been told that the business was very, very confidential. 'Where is there a telephone ?' he asked, to turn the conversation.

He walked and talked soberly, though he could have pranced to the telephone. This was his doing. He was going to share the credit. He was the one who had found the print on the window. He was the one who had found out to whom it belonged.

In a closed phone box he asked for the familiar Granchester number, and while he waited to be put through he mentally rehearsed what he would say. He resolved that he would be airy, terse, casual, just as if this sort of thing happened to him every day.

Granchester spoke to him. He recognized the voice of the police operator.

'Sergeant Bird here,' he said. 'Put me through to Chief Inspector Martineau.'

He waited again, reflecting that it was a pity to waste

this on Martineau. Would it have been better to have phoned Chief Superintendent Clay ?

'The C.I. has just gone through,' said the operator. 'He'll be with you in a minute.'

Then Martineau spoke. 'Well, did you do any good ?'

'Of all the clear impressions I had, sir, none were on the record. Except one.'

'Why didn't you say that the other way round, you bloody fool ? You had my heart in my boots. Whose was the one on record ?'

'Claude Jackman,' said Bird, carefully calm.

'H'm. Very good.'

'But CLAUDE JACKMAN !' Bird shouted. 'Don't you remember him ? Got away with thousands, none of it found ! Escaped from the Moor, never been seen since !'

'All right, don't bellow at me, sergeant,' said Martineau, and there was the ghost of a chuckle in his voice. 'You've done very well. You can come home now.'

'Well,' said Bird in disgust when he had slammed down the receiver. 'Ungrateful, I call it. Dammit, he might have showed a bit of interest.'

.   .   .   .   .

Like Sergeant Bird, Martineau also enjoyed being the bearer of sensational news. He thought that it was time the boss of the C.I.D. knew about Claude Jackman. But first he told Devery, as he went through the main office. 'I've just got the griff from Bird,' he said. 'It's Jackman, all right. I hardly dared hope it would be.'

'So now we know who Bashful is,' said Devery with satisfaction. 'If he's still in town, we'll get him.'

Martineau nodded. He went on to Clay's office.

The chief superintendent was alone, checking reports. 'Hello,' he said. 'How's the leg ?'

'Doing all right, I think, sir. No throbbing.'

'Family all right ?'

168

'Taking everything into consideration, they're fine. Julia has good nerves.'

'I'm glad to hear it. What's new ?'

'I've got a tale to tell you, and with your permission I'll begin at the beginning.'

'Get on with it, then.'

'Mick McQuade saw some service in Liverpool before he came here. Did you know that ?'

'Better than you. His wife was a Granchester girl. Her parents were in poor health, and she wanted to live somewhere near them, to look after them a bit. So Mick transferred to this force.'

'When he was on the beat in Liverpool he arrested a man called Claude Jackman. Remember him ?'

'I do indeed. As far as I know, he's still wanted.'

'He is. And Sergeant Bird found his finger-prints in Granchester last night. He's been checking them. Just phoned from Wakefield.'

Clay sat very still. 'Claude Jackman,' he breathed. 'My word, if we can get him !'

'We must get him,' said Martineau. He went on to explain why he believed that Jackman was the man who was trying to murder him. He told of the man who drank King's Peg, and of his association with Lennie Leroy. 'So all we've got to do now is find him,' he concluded.

'Right,' said Clay briskly. He rubbed his hands. 'If he's still in this town in an hour's time, he won't get out. We'll cover all roads, railway stations, bus stations and the airport. And the docks, of course. I shall want about twelve hundred pictures of Jackman. Every man will get his description immediately. Surely somebody on this force must know the man by sight.'

'Maybe, but under another identity. He's had something like twelve years to get established as somebody else. The men won't suspect somebody like that.'

'They'll be *told* to suspect somebody like that,' Clay

snapped. 'Have you got this Leroy woman under observation ?'

'Yes, sir. There's just a chance she might lead us to him.'

'Good. Now we'll keep this tight. Inside this force, and no man must breathe a word to either Press or public. The man who does, I'll have his head. We don't want to frighten Jackman into complete hiding.'

'Strange how he stayed in this town when he found that there were two policemen here who knew him.'

'It's a big town. He appeared as a man of property, and from the start he moved at a social level where policemen don't expect to find criminals. But if he's still in this town, he's had it now. He's ours. I'd better be getting busy on it.'

'There's one other little thing,' said Martineau, and he told Clay about Sylvia Paris and her shares, and about his subsequent inquiry. 'I shall get to know something more this afternoon,' he said.

The head of the C.I.D. frowned in thought. 'And you say she's knocking about with Dixie Costello ?' he said seriously. 'She wants to be careful. Leon Crow told me that fire at G.T. was an arson job. He said Costello touched some of the candle money. I didn't believe him, and I've no intention of re-opening the case unless I get some definite evidence, but, by Jove, that woman wants to be careful. If she gets to know something he doesn't want her to know, it might be dangerous for her.'

'She's old enough to look after herself, I think.'

'Well, we'll see,' said Clay. 'Leave me now, and let me be getting on with this thing.'

Martineau returned to his own office, where Devery joined him. The sergeant obviously wanted to talk about Claude Jackman.

'The boss has taken over, so I'm not going to be as busy as I thought I'd be,' Martineau told him. 'Very soon the entire force will be looking for Bashful Claude. Which means that you and I had better get out of the way for an hour, or else Clay might make us spend the day watching the trains go out. We'll toddle round to the Northland and have just the odd one, then we'll have something to eat, then we'll ring in and see what's happening. Clay will have got everything covered by that time, and we'll be left free. Come on, let's vanish.'

They went out, and as they walked towards Lacy Street Devery said, 'I wonder how McQuade, from a moving taxi, recognized a man in a car going in the opposite direction, when he hadn't seen him for about twelve years and didn't expect to see him.'

'I've been thinking about that, and I'm more and more inclined to the belief that we can't afford to forget the Bassey case altogether. On the face of it, for McQuade, a wanted man came unexpectedly out of the past. On the face of it, also, it was mighty sharp of him to have recognized that man as he flashed past. He wasn't supposed to be actually working on the Bassey case when he spotted his man, so we assume his man had nothing to do with the Bassey case. That may be a wrong assumption.'

'But there is now no visible link with the Bassey case. Furthermore, everyone connected with the case has been seen and officially interviewed, either by McQuade or yourself.'

'Everyone that we *know* to be connected with the case. Someone, some broker for instance, may have been nominally involved on behalf of some client who was really involved. And when I think of a nominee I think of William Stanton Hope and his backdoor clients. The man who had been drinking brandy and champagne in Hope's office was probably Jackman and, because of the brandy and champagne, a regular and valued client.'

'I see the drift of your thoughts.'

'Drift is right. Ever since Jackman's name cropped up

171

I've thought of this thing. We know for a fact that McQuade was working on the case of a dishonest or criminally negligent stockbroker. We also have a reasonable suspicion that McQuade was murdered by Jackman, who was also a dishonest stockbroker. By the very nature of their work, stockbrokers must be honest and trustworthy. In all my career I only remember two who got into trouble with the police. One is Bassey, the other is Jackman. And they are both connected with McQuade. The coincidence is too much. Jackman must be mixed up with the Bassey case somehow.'

'That still doesn't account for McQuade spotting Jackman in a moving car.'

'I think it does. I think it was the car itself. During his investigations McQuade had seen the car in some circumstances which aroused his interest, but he had never seen the driver. When he saw the car coming towards him last Monday night, he made sure of seeing the driver clearly. And he saw him so clearly that he recognized him as Jackman.'

'That's a feasible guess, sir, I must admit.'

'It's the best I can do on an empty stomach,' said Martineau.

More guesses shortened the journey to the Northland Hotel, but Devery's were not very constructive. He was too keenly aware of people and traffic. In his opinion, the danger to Martineau was now greater than ever. He was relieved when they entered the hotel, and even so he stood at Ella's bar in a position where he could see the door.

Ella welcomed both men with equal friendliness. There was no sign that her heart had leaped when she saw Devery. There were not many customers in the bar, but when she had served them with drinks she said, 'House full today.'

'What do you mean, Ella ?' Martineau asked.

'Two in the cocktail bar. One in the phone box in the lobby.'

The inspector went to take a cautious look. Sylvia Paris and Dixie Costello were in the cocktail bar. Lennie Leroy was in the telephone box. Either she was listening to someone who was speaking to her, or she was waiting for her call to be answered. She looked anxious and unhappy, Martineau thought.

As soon as Martineau stepped out of her bar, Ella said to Devery in a low voice, 'You'll come for me again tonight, darling ?'

'I hope so,' he responded. 'But I may not be able to. I mean that honestly. I may be very busy.'

'If you're very late, come to my place.'

'But it might be three o'clock in the morning.'

'Come at three o'clock then,' said Ella. Her hand moved along the bar towards his. She slipped a latch-key under his fingers. 'Don't worry, my love,' she said. 'You'll never get into trouble through me.'

Then Martineau returned. 'Drink your ale,' he said to Devery. 'We'd better get out of here. There's Lennie Leroy and I don't want her to set eyes on us.'

They went out. They had another drink and a modest meal in a pub which catered for white-collar workers. Then Martineau ventured to "ring in." There was no news, but he did learn that Clay had gone into the canteen for a meal. This meant that the superintendent had given his orders, made his dispositions, set his men.

Martineau returned to Devery. 'We're safe,' he said. 'We can go in if we like. We don't have to, though.'

'I am loth to remind you,' said Devery. 'But we both have a backlog of paper work.'

The inspector nodded sadly. He hated the sight of an empty report form. 'I suppose we might as well be getting some of it done,' he said. 'At least we'll be on the spot if the job breaks.'

So the afternoon was spent in the dull compilation of fact, with never a surmise or a theory to bring life to it.

Then just before five o'clock Devery went to see William Taylor. He was admitted to Taylor's office at once. The old gentleman greeted him with a smile.

'Well, I've got some information, Sergeant,' he said. 'Though I don't know whether you'll find it to your liking.'

'If it's accurate it will do, sir,' said Devery, smiling also.

'Good. I shall refrain from giving you actual figures, because at this stage I don't think you will need them. You're more interested in personalities than figures, I believe.'

'Any information at all, Mr. Taylor,' the detective murmured.

'Well, here it is. Eight days before the fire, Sylvia Paris owned a large number of Granchester Textile ordinary shares. Lionel Hart owned a smaller number of similar shares. Fourteen days later their names were not on the register. Neither of them owned any shares. And today neither of them own any shares.'

'What about other people? Somebody must have bought those shares.'

'There had been other transactions, mostly small ones. But a new name on the register was William Stanton Hope. He showed up with almost as many shares as Mrs. Paris and Mr. Hart had sold.'

'In other words, he was the buyer.'

'That would appear to be the case. The numbers of the certificates support such a conclusion. He still has them, by the way.'

'Could Mr. Hope be a nominee, fronting for somebody?'

'Yes, he could be.'

'Thank you, Mr. Taylor. Anything else to tell me?'

'Not at the moment, Sergeant.'

Devery put away his notebook. He thanked Mr. Taylor again, and departed. On the way back to Headquarters he remembered that he had promised himself a visit to Traffic, which was the departmental name of the motor patrol. Traffic was housed over the police garages and workshops, which were a little distance from Headquarters. He went there, and walked up the stairs. He met a sergeant he knew.

'Out !' said the sergeant with make-believe insolence. 'Out, I say. No civvies allowed in here.'

'Frightened you, did I ? Scared I'll see all the work you don't do ?'

'Work ? You flatties don't know the meaning of the word. While your shower sits in a ring playing ha'penny nap, our boys are out scouring the city.'

'My goodness. Whatever for ?'

'For this bloke Jackman. Claude Jackman. Of course you won't have heard. You ought to look at the book once in a while.'

'It's your book I want to look at.'

'Ours ? No fear. You're not nosing in here. Go and see if you can find somebody pinching a cauliflower in the market.'

'Accidents I'm interested in. Accidents during the last few days. Since last Monday, in fact.'

'We had a bad week last week. Four fatals. I don't know how many of the other sort.'

'What were your fatals ?'

'Two on Tuesday, a kid at Churlham and an old woman in Bishopsgate. An elderly man at eleven o'clock Friday night, in Russell Street. Another old boy a-Saturday noon in Spring Street, on a pedestrian crossing.'

'The Saturday one was Leon Crow, the fence. Who was your Friday night customer ?'

'Now you're asking something. It's a sticky one, and I'm glad it isn't mine. A man we've since identified as Roland Bemis. About sixty years old. He was found dead in the street. He'd been hit by something, and hit proper. He stank of liquor, and might have been drunk when he was hit. We have no details about that yet. The spot in the road where he was found isn't too well lighted. The driver who bowled him over might not be aware of it, but more likely he knew what he'd done and didn't stop. We've circulated it, of course, and made all the usual inquiries at garages and repair shops. But there's nothing doing, and never a damn witness have we found.'

'Who identified the man as Roland Bemis ?'

'His landlady, I believe. I don't know too much about it. Just a minute, I'll see if the inspector still has the report in his office.'

He went to the door of the inspector's office and knocked. He entered, and a minute later he came out carrying a small file of reports and statements. The inspector on duty in Traffic also appeared in the doorway of the office.

'Any help you can give us with that, Devery, we'll be glad of it,' he called.

'Oh, certainly, sir,' the C.I.D. man replied. 'But I'm only following a vague sort of hunch.'

'Well, good luck with it,' the inspector said, and he went back into his office.

Devery perused the file. Roland Bemis had lived in cheap lodgings in Rubber Street. According to his landlady, he had had no regular occupation. She understood that he had spent many years in the East, where he had been a tea planter.

'Well, blow me down !' said Devery, and his voice trembled with excitement. The other sergeant watched him closely.

Devery read the description of the dead man. Height five feet eleven inches, thin, grey-haired. Aquiline features. About sixty years old.

'Where is he, at the mortuary ?' he asked.

'I suppose so. We haven't been able to find any of his relations.'

'I want a car. Any old car that'll go.'

'All our cars will go,' said the sergeant, as he reached for the telephone.

In the car, driving himself, Devery did not immediately go to the mortuary. He went to Headquarters, to Records. To fit into the pattern, Roland Bemis had to have a police record—not in Granchester, but somewhere near.

The sergeant hunted through the file of record cards and found the name he sought. Roland Bemis had a recent conviction for false pretences in the nearby town of Boyton. He also had a long string of similar convictions in the Metropolitan Police District, that is to say, London. The Boyton police had sent these details to Granchester because Bemis had a Granchester address.

Devery jotted down the number of the record card and went to the files. Boyton had obliged with a file on Roland Bemis, with a photograph. He stared at the clear picture, and the picture stared back at him. It was, he afterwards told a certain lady friend, like promotion staring him in the face.

He signed for the file and took it with him to Martineau's office. There was no answer to his knock. He went to the canteen, and found the chief inspector having a snack. He ordered tea for himself.

'Well ?' came the question. 'Did you see Taylor ?'

'Yes,' said Devery. He tucked the Bemis file under his arm and took out his pocket-book to read the details of Taylor's information.

'So William Stanton Hope got the shares,' said Martineau thoughtfully. 'And he could be a nominee. Ah well, I don't suppose we'll be able to make anything out of that.'

Smiling a little, Devery fanned his tea with the Bemis file.

'What's up with you ?' the other man growled. 'What have you got there ?'

'A file ? On a man called Roland Bemis.'

'Who's he ?'

'You'll be surprised who he is. But I'd better begin at the beginning.'

'Oh, do,' urged Martineau with heavy sarcasm.

'Very good. After your little accident on Sunday, and after Leon Crow's accident on Saturday, it occurred to me that the motor vehicle might be somebody's favourite murder weapon. So I called in Traffic to see what other accidents there had been. I found that a man called Roland Bemis had been killed on Friday night.'

'So ?'

Devery opened the file. 'This is Roland Bemis,' he said.

Martineau gaped at the picture. Then he closed his mouth tight. 'Lionel Hart,' he said softly through his teeth. 'He ran a ringer on us. He diddled us with one of the oldest and simplest tricks in the game.'

'So we haven't set eyes on him.'

'For us to see him was the last thing he wanted. Why ? Because he's our client. A pound to a penny he's our man.'

'You'll notice that this man Bemis had a local record. He'd had his name in the paper.'

'Yes, that's how our bashful friend has recruited his help. He kept newspaper cuttings.'

'But he wasn't anonymous to Bemis.'

'No. There was blackmail or danger of blackmail, so Bemis had to be removed when he'd served his purpose.'

'My word, he's ruthless.'

'More than that. He's more than a little barmy, I think. Though normally he should have been safe enough getting rid of Bemis. The victims of fatal accidents don't get their pictures in the paper, and they don't come within the province of the C.I.D. He must have known that. He'd never dream that a C.I.D. man might decide to take a look at a Traffic report. You did well there, Devery. You've located Claude Jackman, and I'll see you get the credit for it.'

178

'Mr. Jackman-Hart, of the Elms, Elms Road, Davidsham. When do we go to see him ?'

'As soon as we get organized. You've got to give me time to get over the shock.'

'Bemis is at the mortuary, and I have a car at the door. Had we better go and have a look at him, just to be sure ?'

'I feel sure already,' said Martineau. 'But we'll go and look.'

16

AFTER A VISIT to the mortuary and a glance at the
dead face of Roland Bemis, Martineau began to make
his arangements for a visit to The Elms, Davidsham.
Though time might be precious, he did not hurry. He was
not *absolutely* certain that Lionel Hart and Claude Jackman were one and the same person, and because of this
he wanted to see Hart before Hart saw him. For this purpose he needed the cover of darkness, and he had to wait
for it. He got his search warrant, earmarked two cars, and
gathered his men. They were good men ; Devery, Ducklin,
Cassidy, Cook, Evans, Jackson, Murray and two drivers
from Traffic who were told to go home and come back in
plain clothes. Those were all the men that Clay could
spare him, but they were also, he thought, all the men
he needed.

Half-past eight was his zero hour, but at 8.20 he received a call from one of the detectives who had been
detailed to act as Lennie Leroy's shadow.

'She slipped me,' came his cry of distress. 'She jumped
on a Number 48 bus and left me standing. While I'm
making this call I'm looking out for a taxi, so I can follow
the bus. I only hope she doesn't get off at the next stop.'

'Where does a Number 48 bus go ?' Martineau asked.

'Davidsham Village is the terminus.'

'Is it indeed ? All right, get your taxi and follow the
bus. It's quite likely that your client will go all the way to
the terminus. Look out for her there.'

'Yes, sir,' said the man, relieved but slightly mystified.
Martineau put down the phone. 'All right,' he said to
the assembled men. 'We'd better start now.'

They went out and piled into the two cars. Martineau
sat beside the driver of the leading car. 'Do you know the
bus route to Davidsham ?' he asked.

'I believe I do,' the man replied. 'It goes direct.'

'Get on to the route and follow it,' the inspector ordered.
'And don't be in too much of a hurry. Just trundle along
and let us enjoy the weather.'

It was certainly not an unpleasant ride. The evening
traffic was not heavy ; the road was good and so was the
car. It was dusk. The air was mildly warm and still, and
when they passed through pleasant suburbs it was occasion-
ally heavy with the scent of blossom. The men smoked,
and the tone and nature of their conversation betrayed
their subdued elation. They counted themselves lucky to
be with Martineau that night. Of all the men who were
seeking Claude Jackman, they were the ones who were
most likely to meet him. Claude Jackman, the only man
who had ever got out of Dartmoor and stayed out, the
murderer of Mick McQuade, the man who had tried to
kill Martineau. No doubt each one of them was praying
that he would be the man who made the arrest.

A mile from the Davidsham bus terminus they saw a
taxicab moving very steadily ahead of them, and distantly
ahead of the taxi they saw a bus.

'Follow and keep well back,' Martineau ordered. 'We're
all going the same way. Miss Leroy can lead the way and
show us where the dogs are, if any.'

'I was transferred from this division a year ago,' said
Evans. 'There were no dogs at The Elms then.'

'Happen Mr. Hart doesn't like dogs since the blood-
hounds chased him across the Moor,' said Martineau. 'Did
you know Hart when you were in this area ?'

'No, sir. I wish I had done. I never saw him at all.'

'I see. When you were around the house at night, no dogs ever barked. Is that it ?'

'That's it, sir,' said Evans.

Martineau also knew the house and the district from his days as a patrol constable, before Lionel Hart had ever seen the place. When the bus finally stopped on the village green at Davidsham he was able to guide his driver round the other side of the green and on the way to Elms Road. This was done while Miss Leroy was still alighting from the bus, and while her police shadow was hurriedly paying his cab driver.

'Now we're at the head of the procession,' said Martineau. 'And we will have time to get into position while Leroy is walking from the village. We'll be able to see how she gets into the place.'

'She's going to have it out with Lionel,' said Devery from the back of the car. 'She's been trying to get him on the phone and he wouldn't answer. He ain't gonna give her the brush-off. No, sir. She don't like it.'

'Lionel will learn that it is always easier to get friendly with a frail lady than it is to get rid of her,' somebody said.

Devery was silent.

The police cars ran along Elms Road. It was tree-lined, with high garden walls on either side. The trees made the indifferent street lighting seem to be even less effective than it was.

The Elms was the second house on the left, and the biggest of the big houses on the long road. The grounds were large, with wide lawns and ancient shrubberies, and with a deep belt of trees to screen the workaday world outside the garden wall.

'Drop us here,' said Martineau, and the two cars stopped in the shadow of a big tree. 'Don't bang those doors,' he warned as the men began to alight.

He sent the cars away, to remain out of sight, but within hearing of a police whistle. Evans, Jackson and

Murray he sent to the back gate of the house ; Evans being appointed as messenger to carry the news of any unexpected happening there. At the front there would be himself, Devery, Cassidy, Ducklin and Cook.

The big wrought-iron front gate of The Elms stood wide open. Martineau reflected that open gates and no dogs were a deliberate sign to the neighbours that here lived a man who had nothing to hide. Or perhaps the man did not like closed gates for the same reason that he did not like dogs.

Cook was posted on the other side of the road, with a big tree to hide behind, in such a position that his signal could be seen from inside the gateway. With his remaining three men, Martineau entered the grounds of the house. Inside the gateway there were trees and shrubs on one side of the drive. They hid among the shrubs, waiting for Cook to warn them of the approach of Lennie Leroy.

But others arrived before Miss Leroy. A car came along the road. As it slowed to turn through the gateway Cook had no time to give warning, but his colleagues had heard it, and they were well hidden when it passed up the drive. It was a black Ford Zephyr, with two people in the front seat. Martineau could not distinguish who they were, or of what sex.

He did not hear the car stop, but distantly he heard the banging of car doors : one, two. Then all was still, except for a very faint rustling of leaves which was like an almost inaudible, long-drawn sigh. It was now quite dark ; a glorious, starry spring night.

Cook did not need to give warning of Lennie Leroy's approach. The brisk click of her heels on the sidewalk could be heard two hundred yards away. She went through the gateway and marched smartly up the drive, looking neither across the lawns nor at the sable mass of the trees. Obviously she was not afraid of the dark.

Then Cook put his closed fingers over the bulb of his

flashlight and pressed the switch. Martineau saw, momentarily, a faint pink glow. The ass, he thought without irritation. Of course there was somebody following Leroy : none other than her official shadow, Detective Constable Holden, who would have to be intercepted and given new instructions.

A figure slipped through the shadowed side of the gateway like a wraith. It was a man, but it was not Holden. This stranger was not as tall or as broad as Holden. He passed within six feet of Martineau, but, screened by leaves, the inspector could not see his face without moving and betraying his own presence. The man went on up the drive, apparently following Miss Leroy.

Then came Holden, cautious and noiseless. He slid quickly round the shadowed gatepost and stood in blackness, looking about him. None of the other policemen moved. Eventually Holden started forward. When he was near Martineau the inspector whispered his name, and showed himself. The startled man, assuming for a moment that he was about to be bushwhacked, jumped away and crouched in a defensive attitude.

'Shhhh !' said Martineau, not moving.

Holden came closer, peering. He relaxed. 'Phew !'

'Who's the man ahead ?' Martineau breathed.

'I don't know, sir,' came the whispered reply. 'He got off the same bus as Leroy. He seemed to be following her, so I followed him.'

'Right. Now you're under my orders. There are five of us here, and three at the back.'

The inspector stepped out of cover as far as the grass verge of the drive. His men joined him, and Cook came flitting across the road.

'Follow me,' he whispered. 'When we get near the house you'll go where I point, without speaking. When you're on your own you'll use your common sense and act according to events.'

He led the way, walking on short grass near the drive, and keeping in the shadows as much as possible. His men followed him silently, in single file.

Fifty yards up the drive there was a bend, and here there were trees on both sides. From there the house could be seen, and Martineau perceived that the clump of trees on his right had been planted merely to hide the building from people who looked in at the gate. But for these trees he would have been able to watch the progress of Miss Leroy and her unknown follower all the way from the gate to the house. There was a big porch light burning over the front door, and further along the terrace in front of the house brilliant light poured from a large, open french window. From the asphalt forecourt of the house the drive continued below the terrace, running parallel with it, going on and back so that it was also the perimeter of a rectangular lawn with rounded corners. This rectangular lawn was bathed in light which faded on further lawns and then became lost among the surrounding trees.

In the middle of the terrace, opposite to the french window, were half-a-dozen wide, shallow steps. At the foot of the steps stood a black car, presumably the Zephyr which had been driven to the house a few minutes ago. Martineau was in time to see Lennie Leroy go up the steps and enter the house. He could not see the man who followed her.

He stopped. His men could now see him clearly in silhouette, and they stopped also. He stood at gaze, looking towards the terrace. He noticed two spherical clipped box trees in big stone tubs, one on each side of the french window. Then he saw movement on the little grassy slope which ran down from the terrace to the drive, and a sort of concerted sigh behind him told him that the others had seen it also. The man he sought was crawling rapidly towards the terrace steps on hands and knees.

The scuttling figure reached the foot of the steps. It darted across and continued along the further slope of grass until it was lost in the darkness beyond. It was then, on the edge of that further darkness, that Martineau noticed something else on the terrace. This was a gathering of objects which looked like a table and some chairs.

He waited, and then he saw his man again, the white face of him as he slunk along the front of the house to the french window. Then he was hidden by the box tree on that side of the window. He had reached his listening post.

Martineau silently cursed the man. He was in the way. He was lurking where Martineau wanted to be. He would get himself spotted, be the cause of an alarm, ruin everything.

Suddenly a light appeared in a bedroom window. It went out. Another light appeared for a few seconds, and was extinguished. In room after room light appeared and disappeared. Somebody was making a quick search of the house ; not looking for jewellery or money, but for people.

The inspector turned to his men. With gestures and brief whispered instructions he sent them to their posts. They stole away along the edge of the trees. Only Holden was told to remain where he was, watching the drive.

Also keeping in the shadow of the trees, Martineau made his way to the back of the house. The backyard was partly surrounded by outbuildings—garage, potting sheds, store sheds, and the like. On the other side of the backyard wall greenhouses glimmered in the starlight. There were trees beyond, but they were not big trees. The orchard, he presumed. The orchard where spraying equipment was sometimes used.

It was a three-car garage. The big main doors were closed, and could not be opened without noise. He looked in black shadow for a side door, and saw a man standing there, watching him. He also stood still. The man came forward. It was Evans.

'All quiet ?' the inspector whispered.
'Not a soul stirring, sir.'
'Have you looked in the garage ?'
'Yes. Two cars in there.'
'What sort ?'
'A Rover and a Bristol.'
'Black Rover ?'
'Black or very dark blue, sir.'
'Can you immobilize those cars without noise ?'
'I can let the tyres down.'
'All right. Do that.'
'Yessir.'

Martineau went on his way, round the house. He came
to the front corner, and looked along the terrace. Light
still streamed from the french window. Crouched behind
the box tree, the stranger now had his back to him. Nearer
were the table and chairs he had noticed before. The table
was large, round, and solid looking. Evidently Lionel Hart
liked to have his breakfast out of doors on fine mornings.

There were a few steps leading to the end of the terrace.
Martineau went up the steps, and moved along close to
the house. As he drew nearer to the source of light, he
realized that he would be visible to the cordon of men who
stood out there in the dark. That was an advantage. If the
unknown man escaped him, they would see what had
happened and they would know what to do.

He walked as quietly as possible, but sure enough there
had to be a small piece of broken lime mortar on the terrace,
and sure enough he had to put his foot on it. It crunched
under his weight ; a slight sound, but as loud as a dropped
brick to him. The man who crouched beside the box tree
sprang to his feet and turned with the agility which high
nervous tension can produce. He was recognized. Barry
Hill was his name, if Martineau remembered rightly.

The policeman, clearly visible to Hill, put a finger to
his lips and raised a fist as big and hard as a pulley block.

His signal was as plain as a spoken message. If you make a sound I'll knock your head off your shoulders.

Hill nodded. Martineau moved in, and quickly and silently searched him for weapons. He found none. He turned the young man round, and indicated by pressure that he should resume his former position. They both crouched beside the box tree.

No sound of voice or movement came out through the french window, and Martineau began to think that there was nobody in the room. Then there was the noise of a closing door, and an irritable utterance in a voice he knew. He knew it well, but the man beside him knew it better.

'I've looked in every damned pantry and closet in the place, and there isn't a sign of him,' Dixie Costello complained. 'Where the devil is he ? He can't just have gone off and left this glass door wide open and all the lights on. And besides, where's the housekeeper or the butler or whoever runs this joint ?'

'There's one place you haven't looked, Richard,' said Sylvia Paris. 'That locked room there. The study.'

Dixie's voice became less irritable, more conciliatory. Martineau thought : So she's got him that way, eating out of her hand. He reflected that it would last just so long, and then Dixie would eat the hand as well.

'Look,' Dixie was saying patiently. 'I've knocked and he don't answer. I've looked through the keyhole and the room's in darkness. I've looked through the window and thick curtains are drawn. He won't be sitting in there in the dark.'

'He might be, if he doesn't want to meet you.'

Dixie did not answer that one. The tone of his voice changed. '*You* know where he is. Where is he ?'

Lennie Leroy answered, 'I tell you I don't know.'

'What are you doing here, anyway ?'

'That's none of your business. What are *you* doing here ?'

'I want to have a word with Mister Lionel Hart.'

'And does she want a word with him, too ?'

'What do you mean by "she"? Are you referring to this lady ? If you want to know, I'm here on her behalf. I'll get what we've come for if I have to shake it out of him.'

'Richard !' There was a little reproach and a lot of warning in the exclamation.

'Oh, don't worry, my dear. I never sing the wrong tune.'

'Talking of shaking people is no way to behave when you're moving into society,' said Miss Leroy. 'Besides, he might shake you.'

'Him ? Pah !'

There was a tinkle of malicious laughter. 'I can't help it,' said Miss Leroy. 'It's so funny. Dixie Costello the knight errant. Sir Galahad Costello.'

'You can cut that out !' Dixie snapped. 'I don't take that sort of lip from bints like you. You can't afford to give it, either. You'll soon be wanting some help if your fancy man has left town.'

'Why would he do that ?'

'Oh, I can think of reasons. The coppers might be after him.'

'Why ?'

'Because he might have been up to something. He's a crook. I know at least one job he was in.'

'I don't believe you,' said Leroy, but there was enough resentment in her voice to indicate that she did believe.

'Please yourself,' said Dixie, unconcerned.

'And is that the way you're going to shake him, by blackmailing him.'

'Certainly not. I never touch the black. I'm just going to make him do what's right by this lady. I've never come copper in my life, but I'm going to make an exception of Hart if he don't give this lady what she is entitled to.'

189

'If you come copper on Lionel, I'll come copper on you.'

Dixie laughed. 'Lover boy's been talking to you. Take no notice. Come to think of it, I might tell Lionel about him.'

'If you do, you'll be sorry.'

'You can't touch me, Lenny. I'm clean. I'm not responsible for what the lad did. He didn't do it under my orders.'

'You made him hand over the money to you.'

'Did he tell you that? You don't want to believe everything you hear.'

'It's true.'

'He was working for me, but not when he did that job. I don't allow that kind of thing. He only saved himself from getting his kisser nicked by offering me the cash as soon as he knew I'd got the griff. But I didn't take it. I made him give it to charity.'

Leroy scoffed at that. 'Charity begins at home,' she said. 'I know you.'

'You don't know me well enough. You don't see me getting mixed up in that sort of lark. Not when there's a party in it who's practically a stranger. I found out all about that. I made the boy tell me. If I'd been a blackmailer, I could have made plenty out of it.'

'Maybe you made some money out of shares.'

'I didn't. I was too late for that. You can't touch me, Lennie. I'm in the clear. All you can do is get your boy friend put in stir. Both of your boy friends, maybe.'

Outside, the listening men waited for a name and a crime to be mentioned. One waited with dread, the other with grim anticipation and a certain amount of pity. The pity was not for the man beside him, whose name he expected to hear at any moment, but for the man's sweetheart. It would be all for the best eventually, but it would be hard for her to lose her prospective husband so soon after she had lost her father.

But neither the name nor the crime was mentioned, and in any case Dixie would not have been the one to mention either. Suddenly he lost patience.

'We can't wait here all night,' he said. 'Let's beat it, my dear. I'll have Hart located tomorrow, and then I'll talk to him. If he's left town, I can still put my finger on him. I got contacts everywhere.'

'Very well, Richard,' said Mrs. Paris. 'Though I do wish we could look in that locked room. Couldn't we get the door open with something ?'

'No blasted fear ! That's breaking and entering. At this time of night it's burglary.'

'Not if it isn't done with felonious intent.'

'Ha ! Now she's teaching me the law. Listen, Sylvia, I knew more about that sort of thing when I was ten years old than you'll ever know. And I knew more about the police. I'm not just an ordinary geezer who goes to work in an office and thinks the cops are a shower of holy men. I'm Dixie Costello. If the coppers nailed me for breaking into a room in this house I could shout about felonious intent till I was black in the face. How would it look, I ask you. I come here on a social visit but the owner of the house don't seem to be around. So I search the house and don't find him, and don't find nothing else either. So just to make sure he ain't at home I break into the room where he keeps his cigars and maybe his money. Coo, the coppers would laugh theirselves silly at me.'

'But you have two witnesses.'

'Lenny and you ? My liberty in the hands of two of the unpredictable sex ? Hush, Sylvia, hush. We don't break no doors down, that's definite. I sweat to think of it. The coppers would get me the longest stretch they could. And incidentally, my dear, do you know the maximum sentence for burglary ?'

'No, Richard. I don't.'

'Life imprisonment, sweetheart. Life imprisonment.'

Outside, Martineau grinned as he listened. Dixie had a fairly accurate knowledge of the feelings of the police towards him. He knew that they had been waiting for years for him to make a mistake.

'Right,' Dixie said briskly. 'Now that's settled, let's go.' Then he seemed to hesitate before he spoke again. 'Can we give Lennie a lift back to town, do you think ?'

'Please yourself, it's your car,' said Mrs. Paris coolly. 'As far as I'm concerned, she can walk.'

'I wouldn't ride to the same funeral with you,' Leroy spat.

'Dearie me, animosity,' said Dixie. 'We'd better be leaving you. Come along, my dear.'

Martineau pressed a heavy hand down on Barry Hill's shoulder. He held the shoulder firmly. Both men crouched lower as Dixie and Mrs. Paris stepped out on to the terrace. The man and the woman passed without seeing them. Dixie, no doubt feeling, as Miss Leroy had remarked, that he was getting into society, took the lady's elbow with exaggerated care as they walked down the steps. At the car he pulled open the door with a flourish, and helped her to get in.

'I'd much prefer to be driving you in my Rolls,' he said. 'But I don't use it when I'm on any sort of business. It's too noticeable. Shall we drive to your place ?'

Martineau did not hear the reply. Dixie got into the car, started the engine, and switched on the headlights. The inspector watched the sweep of those headlights as the car moved round the rectangular lawn. It did not reveal any of his men to him. Apparently they were well hidden.

The sound of the car died away. There was stillness inside and outside the house. On the terrace not even the rustling of trees could be heard. Martineau waited and wondered. Suppose the Leroy girl went away after a little while, and nothing happened. Suppose there *was* nobody in the locked, darkened room. Suppose the whole thing was a waste of time, with Claude Jackman alias Lionel Hart at the other end of the country or on the high seas or flying through the sky.

In self-defence, Martineau refused to believe that Hart had gone away and left doors open and lights burning. The man could not yet know that the police were aware of his dual identity. He would not leave the house like this, to provoke curiosity and enquiries. He was still around the place, somewhere.

The probability was that Hart had seen Costello and Mrs. Paris before they saw him. Not wishing to meet them he had stepped quickly into his study, locking the door and then remaining there in darkness. He had waited, surmising that Costello would soon lose patience and go away. Listening at the door, he had become aware of Lennie Leroy's arrival. Police observers had seen Leroy make repeated unsuccessful attempts to contact somebody by public telephone. Those were calls which Hart had failed to answer. Worried and perhaps desperate, she had made her way to his house, probably in defiance of strict orders from him. She would want money, or she would want to know why he was avoiding her, or she would want him to stay with her, or take her with him. He was her livelihood.

He would know all about that. Now, he only remained in hiding because he wanted her to go away without seeing him.

So reasoned Martineau. If Hart was still in the house, he was in the locked room. So what was there to wait for ?

Still, he remained where he was. He wasn't quite satisfied. He had a feeling that he had missed something. He thought about the matter, and when he perceived that which had eluded him he felt as foolish as if he had been caught stooping at a keyhole. Of course ! The open french window and the beautiful night. Hart had stepped out on to the terrace to breathe the cool night air. He had taken a stroll around the grounds. He had seen the arrival of Costello and Mrs. Paris, and wishing to avoid them he had taken to the cover of the trees. He had observed the arrival of Lennie Leroy and of Barry Hill. And worst of all he had seen Martineau himself walk along the terrace. He was probably out there now, standing a little way beyond the cordon of plain clothes men, watching his own house from behind a tree. Possibly he had seen some of the men move to their allotted posts. That could be the position exactly.

Assuming that theory to be the correct one, would Hart flee immediately ? Could he ? Probably he had only a few pounds and a cheque book in his pocket, but a cheque book might be all he needed. *If* he dared go to his bank in the morning.

That's a point, Martineau thought. If I miss him tonight, I'll have every bank in Granchester covered tomorrow.

With Barry Hill crouching trapped and unhappy beside him, the inspector pondered. The absence of servants bothered him. Costello had stated there wasn't a soul in the place. Well, a house like that could have been run by a staff which did not "live in," but it wasn't likely. It *was* likely that Hart was getting ready to depart hence, and he was doing it in such a way that there would be no neighbourly curiosity, and consequently no newspaper articles headed "Disappearance of Wealthy Bachelor." He had paid off his servants and sent them away. He had perhaps even made arrangements for his house to be sold. He had told his friends and associates that he was going to take a long holiday, or that he was going to live in South Africa. He would do it that way if he still believed that the police did not suspect him of anything at all.

But he was going away because his nerve was beginning to fail him, bold man though he might be. Two narrow escapes would make him feel that the police were getting near to him. He would be in possession of getaway money.

194

The money would be in the house, in that locked room.

So, Hart might be hiding in the locked room, waiting for Lennie Leroy to go away and believing that there wasn't a policeman within a mile of him, or he might be out there among the trees, knowing that the game was up. Knowing that, he would have to come back to the house for his getaway money. To do that, he would have to wait until the police had searched the place and gone away.

Very well, that was what the police would appear to do. Martineau stood erect. He stepped into the blaze of light from the french window, taking Hill with him. He did not speak, but stood with his back to the house and gave the "close in" signal. He wondered if his men remembered their field signals. Apparently they did. They closed in from their various points, moving eerily out of the darkness towards the light. When the nearest was about twenty yards away he gave them the halt signal. They halted. He beckoned individually to Devery, Cassidy, and Cook. They came forward and climbed the steps. In silence, Martineau took Cook's hand and put it on Barry Hill's shoulder. Cook nodded, and let the hand stay where it was.

Martineau whispered to Devery, 'You once told me you could open a door. Now's your chance to prove it.'

He went through the french window, with Devery and Cassidy at his heels. The room which he entered appeared to be some sort of lounge or drawing-room. Lennie Leroy was sitting upright on the edge of an armchair. She stared at him. She was white-faced, and there was fear in her eyes. She was afraid that she had led the police to Lionel Hart, or else she was afraid that Hart would believe she had. Martineau gave her the same signal for silence that he had given to Barry Hill.

He went to the further door of the room and looked along a lighted interior passage, thus making sure that Hart's study did not have a door giving access to the passage. He returned to Devery, and pointed to what was obviously the locked door. The whole idea of his silent pantomime was to make the man who might be in the study think that it was Lennie Leroy who was forcing the door.

Miss Leroy made further silence unnecessary. 'Look out, Lionel !' she called. 'It's the police !'

'Shut up,' said Martineau coldly. And to Devery, 'You said you could use a loid. Let's see you open that door.'

Devery nodded. He went to the door and tried it. Then he looked at the lock. It was a latch lock. 'All right if it isn't deadlocked, sir,' he murmured.

'Jump aside as you throw the door open,' came the order. 'Then Cassidy and I can dash in.'

Devery took out the small note-case in which he carried his warrant card. When his authority was challenged it was his habit to produce the note-case and let it fall open to display the card behind its transparent shield of strong celluloid. Now he removed the celluloid and applied it to the lock.

Perhaps he was not so clever with a "loid" as he had pretended to be, but after a few attempts he managed to work the springy, flexible thing round the tongue of the lock. He turned the door-knob, and simultaneously pushed the door and whipped out the celluloid. The tongue of the lock was pulled back just far enough and long enough for the door to open.

As Martineau rushed into the room Devery put his hand through the doorway and found the light switch, his idea being that a man who had been sitting in darkness would be at a momentary disadvantage when a sudden light appeared. But when he entered, Martineau and Cassidy were looking round in disappointment. 'Nobody in here,' said Cassidy.

The three men searched the room. It was a comfortable, rather shabby room, well stocked with liquor and good cigars. They found a locked safe, and that was all.

If the room held cash or incriminating papers, then they were in the safe. 'Maybe we can have it opened later,' said Martineau.

'No gun,' said Devery.

'No,' the inspector sighed. 'It's to be hoped he hasn't got it in his pocket.'

They returned to the drawing-room, and found that Cook had taken Hill in there. Hill and Miss Leroy sat facing each other, but Hill was staring at the carpet and Leroy with raised head and set face gazed out into the night. Martineau stood and looked from one to the other.

'You three men take a smart and careful canter round the house,' he said. And when Cassidy showed surprise, 'Inside, I mean. I'll stay with these people.'

When the men had gone, he turned to Hill. 'Now then, Barry,' he said. 'What are you doing here ?'

The young man nodded in the direction of the girl. 'I saw her on the bus, and I followed her.'

'Why ?'

'To see what she was up to.'

'What could she have been up to that was any concern of yours ?'

Hill did not reply.

'You fool !' snapped Miss Leroy. 'The police were watching you, and you went and led them here.'

'Hush,' said Martineau. And to Hill, 'What were you doing on that particular bus ?'

'I was taking a ride in the country, to get some air.'

'I think Tess would have enjoyed that, too. Didn't you ask her to go with you ?'

'No. I wanted to be on my own.'

Martineau regarded the man with tolerant disbelief. He would have been pleased to witness the complete reformation which Hill claimed, and he would have given full credit for it when credit was due. But he had always had doubts, doubts which were fathered by sad experience.

197

He was not cynical. He knew many a man who had fallen
from grace just once, thereby learning his lesson and never
committing another crime. He also knew veteran criminals
who had reformed—after the law had broken them and
left them too old and too tired to risk the law's heavy
punishment any more. But he knew very few young toughs
of Hill's type who had turned honest and stayed honest.
He was sorry about that, but there it was. Young crooks
"going straight" were all potential recidivists to him. Their
good intentions he might admit, but he knew that they
could not withstand the stresses and strains of normal
workaday life. They could not bear economic pressure.
They had not the patience to work and save for what
they wanted. They had not the fortitude and the character
to remain honest. In need, they would not wait and work
and perhaps suffer a little ; they would beg, borrow, or
steal.

'Tess has a home all ready for you to move into,' he
said. 'But I suppose you needed capital to get into some
sort of business. What was the name of the horse ?'

'What horse ?'

'The horse that was going to make you enough, but
didn't.'

'I've give up backing horses.'

'Then was it dice or shemmy ?'

'I don't know what you're talking about.'

'I think you do. You lost your money and you wanted
some more, so that you could have another go. You were
on your way to see Lionel Hart when you spotted Miss
Leroy and followed her. You were going to put the black
on Hart.'

'I wasn't,' Hill protested. 'I was going to ask him to
lend me a pound or two.'

'To lend it or else. How did you come to know Hart,
anyway ?'

Hill saw the trap. He looked down, as if it were a physical thing at his feet. He did not reply.

'Answer me,' Martineau demanded.

'I've said all I'm going to say.' It was Barry Hill the cornered mobster who spoke. 'You can't prove nothing. I have no weapons or house-breaking tools. I was coming to ask Mr. Hart to lend me some money.'

'But you didn't mind spying on Miss Leroy, eh ?'

'That was nothing. When I saw Dixie Costello's car, I thought I'd better not show myself till he'd gone.'

Martineau turned to Leroy. 'Did this fellow introduce you to Hart, or did you introduce Hart to him ?'

The girl was silent. Martineau said, 'Never mind, it isn't important.' He began to pace about. He seemed to be deep in thought, but actually he was wondering if his enemy was out there among the trees, looking into the room and watching him.

Devery, Cassidy and Cook returned. 'The house is deserted,' the sergeant reported. 'There isn't even a cat.'

'How many bedrooms showing signs of recent occupation ?'

'One front bedroom. But all the others are spick-and-span, ready for anybody who wants to sleep in them.'

'What about servants' bedrooms ?'

'Just the same. But drawers and wardrobes are empty.'

'Would you say it looked as if Hart has recently paid off all his staff and sent them away ?'

'I'd say it looked exactly like that, sir.'

'Just as I thought. He's getting ready to run.'

'That's it, sir. Except that he didn't intend to run to-night. He hasn't packed his bags.'

'I'm glad to hear it,' said Martineau. He told the two plain clothes men to stay where they were, and then he took Devery with him on a tour of the outhouses. One big

toolshed was locked, but its windows had not been con-
structed for the purpose of keeping out inquisitive policemen. Devery opened a window with a knife. He climbed
through the opening, and used his flashlight. In a little
while he called, 'Better come and look at this, sir.'

"This" was a cylinder with harness, so that it could
be carried on a man's back. There was a compression
device, and a short pipe with a nozzle. 'Yes, that's it,' said
Martineau. 'That's what he used to spray folks' houses
with petrol. Don't touch it. If it still has Hart's finger-
prints on it, that'll be a help.'

They returned to the house, and on the way he told
Devery about his belief that the man he sought was lurking
among the trees, watching and waiting.

'So what do you intend to do ?' came the question.

Martineau did not immediately reply. He knew perfectly well what he *ought* to do. *If* Hart was out there in
the grounds, he had probably counted the members of
the police party. But there were five men whom he had
not seen : Evans, Jackson, Murray and the two drivers.
The thing to do was to smuggle two of those men into
the house by the back door, and get them into the study
unseen by Hart. This could be done by causing the view
through the french window to be temporarily blocked—
three big policemen happening to stand there in a group,
talking—while the two men slipped through the drawing-
room into the study. There they would conceal themselves.
Then the cars would be called, lights would be put out,
and—apparently—everybody would go away. The two men
in the study would wait in the dark until Hart arrived.

That was the thing to do, and Martineau did not want
to do it. Moreover, he knew quite well that he was not
going to do it. Though he knew his men to be strong and
capable, he was afraid that something would go wrong if
he were not present when Hart was confronted. Also, he
was the one man who could be absolutely sure whether

or not Hart and Jackson were the same person. Also, he wanted to make the arrest himself. He wanted to lay hands on the man who had set fire to his house.

'I'll tell you what we'll do,' he said. 'We'll shut up the house and go away. Then we'll come back.'

'Very good, sir. But there's just one thing. Suppose he makes his move before we get back.'

'He won't. He'll have to reconnoitre first. He'll do that very thoroughly. He won't find anybody. He'll go in then. He'll think we've come to the conclusion that he's left town.'

Devery was silent. The other man knew what he was thinking. He also knew that Devery also understood only too well why the thing was going to be done the way it would be.

'I wish we'd brought a pair of night glasses,' he said.

'We have,' said Devery. 'I put mine in the car, just in case.'

'I wouldn't be surprised if you don't get a bit of promotion out of this job,' said Martineau.

17

ON THE TERRACE of The Elms, standing in the light from the french window, Martineau whistled up his men and his cars. They came, and the men gathered round him. 'There's nothing here,' he said. 'We might as well go.'

After that, he spoke to only one officer in particular. That was Holden, who did not like the orders he received but dared not showed his displeasure.

'I'm putting the Leroy girl and Barry Hill in your charge,' the inspector said. 'You'll take them to Head-quarters and you'll interrogate them about the murder of Inspector McQuade, about their connection with a man called Lionel Hart who lives at this house, and about any-thing else which comes into your head. You'll keep on interrogating them until I give you the word to let them go. I don't want them loose and roaming the streets, you understand ?'

'Yessir,' said the unlucky Holden.

Martineau went into the drawing-room and spoke to the two who sat there. 'Come along. Somebody wants to speak to you at the police station.'

'You can't take me to the police station,' said Miss Leroy. 'I've done nothing. I'm waiting here to see someone.'

'That someone isn't here, and if he comes he won't have time to talk to you. Holden !'

Holden came and took his two hostages to one of the cars. Martineau went through the hall and found that the front door had a mortise lock with a key in it. The french window had a latch lock. He dropped the latch and slammed the door, then went back to the front door, turning out lights as he went. He opened the front door and found that the switch of the porch light was on the porch itself. He locked the door, put the key in his pocket, and turned out the light. Except for the key in his pocket, he had left the house as any policeman would leave a temporarily unoccupied house. There would be nothing in his actions to arouse Hart's suspicions.

Now the front of the house was illuminated only by the stars and by the headlights of cars. The latter were bright enough to show a watcher what was going on, and it was even possible that he might be able to count heads. At an order from Martineau the men piled into the cars ; the inspector, Evans, Holden, Miss Leroy, Hill and a driver in one car ; Devery, Cassidy, Cook, Ducklin, Jackson, Murray and a driver in the other. The second car was very full indeed, and there was much grunting as men tried to make room for their meaty shoulders and by no means negligible buttocks. Then doors were slammed and the cars moved off, down the drive and out of the grounds and along Elms Road.

Martineau had already told Devery how to instruct his driver ; now he began to instruct his own. As the cars turned from Elms Road into the main road through Davidsham, he said, 'I want you to slow to a walking pace while still making the same noise as you're making now. Can you do that ?'

'I think so, sir,' said the driver.

'Good. Someone may be listening, see ? When you slow, Evans and I are going to leave you, but you must not bang any car doors until you're right away down the road. Then you can carry on to Headquarters.'

203

The car slowed. Evans and Martineau alighted. The inspector's sore leg hampered him, and he stumbled and fell. He was up again in an instant, waving the car on. Men were quite literally falling out of the second car : Cassidy rolled, Jackson went down on one knee, Cook spun round and sat down in the road. But there was no noise and nobody was hurt. The cars went on. Both rear doors of the second car were hanging wide open.

The men gathered round Martineau. There were seven of them and, now, he wished he could have had two or three more. Pondering, he considered them. He looked at his watch. The time was five minutes past ten. In half-an-hour the pub on the village green would be turning out its customers. The late buses would be bringing people home from the theatres, cinemas and hotels of Granchester. Until then, the suburban road would be deserted as it was now. There was plenty of time for the men to take up stations without being seen by local residents.

He wasn't sure whether there were four or five big houses on the same side of Elms Road as Hart's house, but he knew that the house was the second along the road. He realized that he would have to cover the entire block of houses and grounds to make sure that Hart did not escape him. He also realized that he could do it with confidence because the seven who waited for orders were all picked men.

'Jackson,' he said. 'You're posted to this end of the back road. Murray, you go to the other end of the back road. Ducklin, you're at the other end, at the front. Cook, you're at this end, at the front. Cassidy, you'll be somewhere near the front gate. You will all be on the opposite side of the road from Elms House, and you should be able to see anything which moves on either back road or front. Nobody who could possibly be Claude Jackman must get past you. Remember that he might come out of any gate, or over the wall at any place. Anybody or anything going

204

in, let it go. Any car coming away from the house must be marked down. Without showing yourselves, get its number and description, get through the Headquarters and have it stopped.'

He paused. The second police car had rolled silently to a stop at the kerb beside him. Its driver, following Devery's orders, had stopped in Davidsham, closed his doors, run round the village green and returned.

Martineau put his hand on the top of the car. 'Here's a car if you should need to chase anybody, and it is also your means of communication with Headquarters,' he said. 'You must all be well concealed, especially you, Cassidy. Don't forget that our man will reconnoitre before he does anything.'

He turned to Evans. 'Did you let those tyres down ?' 'Yes, sir.'

'Right. You'll go back to the garage and keep it under observation. You must be exceptionally well hidden. If our man comes and starts inflating tyres, you will use your judgment as to what to do. You will probably have time to get some help before you tackle him. You'll want to make sure of him, you know. Now then, is all clear ?'

'Yes, sir,' came the chorus in undertones.

'Off you go, then.' The men dispersed. Martineau and Devery were left alone beside the car.

'What now ?' the sergeant asked.

'Got your night glasses ?'

'In my pocket.'

'Good. Come with me.'

They walked along Elms Road as far as the gate of the first house. The gate was closed, but not locked. They entered, opening and closing the gate very carefully and quietly. Walking in the shadow of trees, on grass and bare earth, they made their way to the dividing wall between that place and The Elms. Both gardens were set out in such a way that shrubberies masked the dividing wall, with

205

rising ground up to the wall to give height to the trees and bushes. Thus when they came to the wall they found it to be no more than five feet high.

'We'll take turns with the glasses,' Martineau whispered. 'Keep your eye on the terrace.'

They climbed over the wall, and moved with great care among the trees until they found a good hiding place from which they could look across the lawns and see the front of Lionel Hart's house. Somewhere a church clock chimed the quarter-hour, and then the night was still. They settled down to wait.

·   ·   ·   ·   ·

Martineau stared at the darkened house, with all its windows glimmering in starlight. He did not feel happy. Everything was too uncertain. There was a chance that he might be outwitted. He was making too personal a thing of this. There ought to be two or three men now hiding in the study, and fifty men surrounding the grounds. He was doing this the wrong way. If Claude Jackman escaped, the Chief would be furious, and justifiably so.

Nevertheless, the big inspector did not think of changing his plans. Not only was he seeking the murderer of Mick McQuade, he was seeking the man who burned his house down, tried to kill him, tried to ruin his career. He yearned for physical contact with the man. That was quite wrong, and he knew it. But he had the authority to handle the affair in his own way, and this was the way it would be.

Time passed. A few cars went along Elms Road and Davidsham Road. A few men, loud-spoken and garrulous after an hour or two at the local inn, were heard making their various ways home. Then Davidsham settled down for night.

The men waited. Midnight came. An owl hooted, seeking to make some small creature stir so that its marvellous eyes might see the movement. The night was so quiet that the owl's cry made Martineau's nerves jump. What a way to make a living, he thought. He craved for a cigarette.

Devery, peering through the night glasses, wondered if Ella Bowie would be waiting up for him. She had told him to come, no matter what time he retired from duty. She was keen, all right. Sort of infatuated, he supposed. He did not know how it would all end, and he felt a vague premonition of trouble. She was the wrong kind of girl for an ambitious policeman, but she had told him that he would never get into trouble through her. He was stirred by the thought of her, waiting for him. Dammit, Jackman, make a move. Don't keep us here all night.

Then Devery observed movement on the terrace. For a moment there was a black rectangle where starlight had glittered on the french window. Then the starlight moved as the window was closed. It made a faint path of light across it, and then was still.

'I thought I saw something,' whispered Martineau.

Devery lowered the glasses. 'You did,' he replied. 'Somebody just went in by the french window.' And as Martineau started to get to his feet, 'He may be looking out, to see if anybody makes a move.'

'We'll move to where he can't see us from there, then we'll sneak along the terrace. I'll go in. You'll stay on the terrace in case he gives me the slip.'

'Wouldn't it be better if I came in with you ?'

'No. It's going to be him and me alone, for a start.'

'He'll shoot you,' said Devery.

'He won't. Do as you're told and don't argue. Come on.'

'Just a minute,' said the sergeant, who had not shifted his glance from the terrace. He raised his glasses again. 'Now the french window is open, but nobody has come out.'

'He's gone into the study,' said Martineau with certainty. 'He's left that glass door open because he can't bear to be shut in when he feels there is danger. Fellows who've

207

had a taste of prison are like that. Come on, we're wasting time.'

He led the way, and made straight for the terrace steps. He had a strange feeling as he silently set foot on the terrace. He was walking in the footsteps of Mick McQuade. One week ago McQuade had walked this way to his death. He had crossed the terrace to that open french window on a warm evening in daylight. He may have tapped on the window and called out, but more probably he had not done so. He had wanted to confirm a suspicion and he had strolled into the house. He should never have handled the business that way, but that was the way he had handled it. He had walked in with confidence, not expecting to meet a man with a gun. Martineau did expect to meet a man with a gun. Then what sort of a fool was Martineau ?

He also thought: This first-class bastard nearly burned my wife and child to death.

Conscious that he would be outlined against the lesser darkness of outdoors, Martineau stepped through the opening, into the drawing-room. There was a narrow shaft of light on the floor of the room, coming from the slightly open doorway of the study. He crossed the room silently, and without touching the door he looked into the study. Soft light from a shaded table lamp glowed in there. It shone upon the broad back of a man who crouched at the safe under the window. He was taking things from the safe and putting them into a grip-top leather travelling case.

Martineau pushed open the study door. It made no noise. He stepped into the study. His tall, wide presence there might have caused some change in the position of shadows, or perhaps the hypersensitive sweating man at the safe might have simply sensed him. At any rate, while the policeman was yet too far away to reach him, the man snatched something from the safe and rose to his feet and turned all in one movement. The thing he had snatched from the safe was a gun. *The* gun, Martineau had no doubt. The evidence of murder which was required.

The gun also had a silencer, which explained why a man could be shot in this house without the servants being aware of it.

At first, the man with the gun seemed to be frightened. He put a hand to his mouth, then removed it. The colour which had gone from his face returned in a red tide. His eyes glowed. Martineau recognized him. The man's neck, shoulders and head still had the unmistakable likeness of a bull, so far as a human being can resemble an animal of another species. It was Claude Jackman, without a doubt. Years older, stones heavier, more suffused about the eyes : a middle-aged bull now, but still a formidable one.

'Who are you ?' Jackman asked. His speech was thick, as if he had had a slight cerebral haemorrhage at some time.

This beast, thought Martineau. This beast. He felt the rage rising in him. He controlled it.

'You know who I am,' he said. 'But just to make sure there's no mistake, I am a police officer.'

The man's head went back. His lip curled. He was the picture of insane arrogance. As Martineau had suspected, he was mad. Not certifiably mad, perhaps, but mad all the same. It was the sort of madness which could only show itself in a time of excitement or stress.

'A common policeman !' the madman rasped. 'Get out of here !'

Martineau began to back towards the door.

'Stop !' Jackman said, and Martineau stopped. 'What right have you here ?'

'I have a search warrant.'

'What are you searching for ?'

'Nothing. I've found what I was looking for.'

'And what was that ?'

'You.'

'You intend to arrest me ?'

'Yes.'

The arrogance showed itself. 'No filthy policeman will ever lay hands on me again.'

Martineau did not answer.

'Are you alone ?' Jackman asked.

'No. I'm with you.'

'I do believe you're alone, like the other one was. You'd have this room full of men if you were not.'

Again Martineau did not reply. He was measuring the distance to the lamp. If he could knock that over, or upset the table on which it stood. . . .

'Don't try that,' said Jackman. His teeth showed. 'You know me, of course. You and McQuade were the two who knew me. I owe you something for that day in Liverpool. I'm afraid I shall have to kill you.'

'You won't kill me. I'll break your neck before you can kill me.'

'You never could do that. Stand still !'

Martineau stood.

'Raise your hands above your head. That's better. I'm curious about one thing. How did you find me ?'

'Through a man called Bemis.'

Jackman grinned. It was obvious that he was beginning to enjoy himself. 'I fooled you there, didn't I ? It was a pity about Bemis. Silly little man. After he had served his purpose he became a danger.'

'You killed him, didn't you ?'

'This is not the day of confession. Furthermore, you're wasting my time. Keep still now ! One move, and I'll shoot.'

Jackman knelt. Without shifting his eyes from Martineau, he reached behind him, feeling for the safe. In that position he resumed the business of transferring bundles of paper money from the safe to the leather bag. Martineau thought that he would never get a better chance of kicking the pistol out of the man's hand. He tensed himself.

'I'm watching you,' said Jackman, pushing the gun forward a little.

He emptied the safe of money while Martineau perforce stood still. He pushed the safe door, but did not trouble to close it properly. With one hand he closed the travelling bag. Then he stood up. He was panting, and his face was red.

'All this trouble through you,' he gritted, his voice thickening as rage returned. 'All my life upset again. Why wasn't I left in peace ?'

His face went a darker red and his eyes became more suffused. Veins on his forehead seemed to stand out. He shook with anger and hatred, but the pistol still remained accurately aimed at his enemy's heart.

Martineau's own hatred rose as if to meet the other man's. His feelings were such that he had no fear of imminent death. But he did not lose his head. He wanted to win, and to do so he had to outwit this arrogant killer.

'Don't shoot !' he cried loudly in simulated terror. 'Don't shoot !'

Jackman's expression did not change, but he did pause to say a final word. 'A coward, too,' he mouthed. 'Well, die like——'

There was a great crash behind him, and the big round table from the terrace came in sideways through the window, taking glass and woodwork with it, and sweeping aside the heavy curtains. It did not come into the room slowly, but at a speed which suggested that the man who had launched it had run the width of the terrace with it. It seemed to spin on the top of the safe, and one leg hit Jackman on the back of the head. It knocked him forward. His gun went off and the bullet went into the floor between Martineau's feet. He went forward, head down like a charging bull. Martineau met him halfway, his right fist going down and up in a vicious hook. The collision of fist and face was perfectly timed. Jackman was stopped. He stood

poised for a fraction of a second, knees bent and head back
and eyes turning upward in his head. Then the knees col-
lapsed. He arched forward and fell on his face. Martineau
put his foot on the hand that held the gun, but he had
no need to do it. His fist had felled Jackman as a pole-axe
might fell a bull.

'That was a beauty,' said Devery from the window. He
disappeared, and entered the room by the door. By that
time Martineau had taken possession of the pistol, and was
looking at it. 'It's the proper calibre, at any rate,' he said
as he slipped it into his pocket.

'Are you all right, sir ?' Devery asked.

'Yes. My pants are clean, too, and that's a miracle.
Thanks for saving my bacon. You were right. I was a fool
to meet this character alone. But I've had my smack at
him and I'm satisfied. All I want to do now is see him
hanged for the murder of Mick McQuade.'

Devery bent, and rolled Jackman over, so that he lay
on his back. 'Cor !' he said in awe. 'You've knocked his
face out of shape.'

The face they looked at was dark red. It was contorted,
but on the right side and not the left. As they watched, they
saw the man's left arm and leg move slightly, but not the
right. His breathing was heavy and noisy.

'I hit this side of his face, not that,' said Martineau.
He knelt and raised the man's eyelids. The pupils of the
eyes were unequal in size.

'He's had a stroke,' said Devery.

His colleague nodded. He remembered the man's rage,
and the pulsing veins in his head. He wondered if his own
violent blow had caused the cerebral haemorrhage, but not
aloud, not even to Devery. 'He was ripe for it,' he said.
'Out of condition. Happen he'd started to get like that
character Taylor told us about, drinking champagne and
brandy without the champagne.'

'He won't cause us any trouble when he comes to, at

any rate,' said the sergeant. 'If he's able to talk I'll be surprised.'

He went into the drawing-room and found cushions, with which he propped Jackman's head and shoulders, putting into practice a First Aid catch-phrase which he remembered : "Face red, raise head."

'How about moving him to the sofa in the other room ?' he asked.

'Leave him where he is,' said Martineau callously. 'I'll get the ambulance.'

He used the telephone on the desk. He made several calls, then he went out to the terrace and whistled up his men. One by one they came, their tongues discreetly silent and their faces full of wild surmise when they saw Jackman. No doubt they wondered which of their superiors had put the man so effectively out of the fight. The overturned table, the broken window and the general disorder made the study look as if it had been the scene of a rare old rough-and-tumble.

Before the ambulance arrived, Jackman ceased to breathe stertorously. His face became a grotesque mask, and his colour faded. Martineau and Devery began to fear the worst, but Murray, an acknowledged First Aid expert, could still detect a beating pulse.

In a little while Murray said that the pulse had faded. 'Anybody got a shiny cigarette case, or a little mirror ?' he asked. Nobody had a cigarette case or a mirror.

Then came Dr. Kerry, police surgeon for that division. His face gave no indication of his thoughts as he looked down at Jackman. 'How long has he been like this ?' he asked.

'He had a pulse three minutes ago, sir,' said Murray.

'Mmmm,' said the doctor. He went down on one knee and opened his bag. He prepared a syringe, working quickly and deftly. Then he bared Jackman's forearm and swabbed it, and gave him an injection. He waited, finger on pulse.

The men who watched him were as still as the man on the floor.

At length he rose to his feet. He put away his instruments and closed his bag. 'Not a flicker,' he said. 'The man is dead.'

Devery looked at Martineau. Martineau turned away from everybody and stared out through the broken window. As he saw it, he had killed Jackman, and killed him unnecessarily. When the table came through the window he should have gone for the man's gun, instead of wreaking his fury by smashing his face in. He had avenged Mick McQuade and he had avenged himself, but he had also robbed himself of his own prisoner. He had ruined the job.

How did I know he was going to have a haemorrhage? he asked himself, but in bitter self-reproach. He knew that it was no use trying to put the blame on Jackman for dying. He, Martineau, had done wrong. He had used more than the minimum force necessary to effect an arrest. He had kept hatred in control right until the last moment, and then, when he should merely have disarmed his man, he had given way to it.

The ambulance arrived, and the body was taken away. Chief Superintendent Clay came and went, the Chief Constable came and went, the Assistant Chief Constable came and went. But all the time Martineau remained where he was, staring out into the night. Those men asked questions, but Devery was there to answer. Devery told the story which he intended to tell the Coroner. Jackman had tried to shoot Martineau; Martineau had tried to get the gun away from him; in the struggle Jackman had been knocked down. That was how it looked to him.

The great men listened to Devery, and looked curiously at Martineau. But they did not disturb him. No doubt they had some idea of his feelings, and decided that they could wait to hear his story.

When all the bosses and experts had been and gone—

and in the confusion taking Martineau's police car with them—the inspector was left with his original seven men. They awaited his orders, not talking much and beginning to be just a little bored. He may have sensed their restlessness, because he roused himself from his introspective mood and turned away from the window.

'Some of you open that bag and count those bundles of money,' he said wearily. 'They're in hundreds, I think.'

He pulled open the door of the safe, and carried its contents to the table. The contents were papers—deeds, important letters, insurance policies and the like. He and Devery examined them but the only significant item which they found was a file of newspaper cuttings. The cuttings answered a lot of questions for Martineau. They were accounts of local criminal trials, and the names and addresses of the accused men were given. With a certain foresight, Jackman had been keeping the cuttings for years. Among them Martineau found the names of Bert Preston, Leon Crow, Barry Hill, and Roland Bemis. This, then, was the file which Jackman had consulted when he wanted a crook to do a job for him. Somewhere in it would be the names of the two men who had tried to kill Martineau by running him down on a pedestrian crossing.

The inspector closed the file and pushed the rest of the papers aside for Devery to return them to the safe. He looked at the men who were counting money. They had finished their task, and each man was making a note of the sum in his pocket-book.

'How much ?' he asked.

'Two hundred bundles, sir,' said Ducklin. 'Exactly twenty thousand pounds.'

'All right, you take charge of it, Ducklin. You others see if you can block the window with that round table. But don't damage the table. I'm very fond of it.'

The men grinned, glad to see a slight change of spirit in Martineau. They put the table top into the window

215

frame, and began to support it with other articles of furniture.

The inspector went out to the terrace, and it was then he found that no car awaited him.

He returned to the study and phoned Headquarters. He asked for two cars, and gave orders for Barry Hill and Lennie Leroy to be set free. They could be questioned at another time.

Then he went and latched the french window, handed the file of press cuttings to Evans, and herded his men to the front door, turning out lights as he went. When everyone was out of the building he locked the front door and put the key in his pocket.

He sat down on the front steps to await the arrival of transport, and his men followed suit. 'Gentlemen, you may smoke,' he said. He needed a smoke himself, and the solace of tobacco accelerated his improvement in mood. He reflected that the night's work could have had a more unhappy conclusion. Yes, much more unhappy. There would be no murder trial and no triumphant producing of an escaped convict, but at least Chief Inspector Harry Martineau was still alive and the McQuade job was cleared. The gun in his pocket would do that little thing, he felt certain. Jackman's tacit admission in the matter of Roland Bemis would also be sufficient to write off that case. Three files would be permanently closed, but the file on Claude Jackman as Lionel Hart would still be open. That was an arson case all right, and a big one. But where would the evidence come from ? Jackman was dead, William Stanton Hope was probably guiltless and without guilty knowledge, Barry Hill would not talk himself into trouble, and it was extremely doubtful if Dixie Costello or Lennie Leroy would give any information. "Still," Martineau decided, "we'll give it a try. Reformed or not, if young Hill has done it he ought to pay the price."

Suddenly he chuckled, and his companions turned their

heads to look at him. He was thinking about Mrs. Paris and Dixie Costello. What were they doing now ? Was Mrs. Paris making free of her favours in order to keep Dixie busy on her behalf ? She was flogging a dead horse, all right. She would get nothing back from Hart now.

Then Martineau laughed aloud. Dixie had spoken confidently of finding Hart wherever he went. Dixie had contacts everywhere, so he had said. Many of his old friends would already be in the place where Hart had gone, running the gambling hells and fiddling with the coal ration. But he would not be able to make contact with them. The spiritual side of Dixie was strictly out of the bottle.

Feeling much better, Martineau breathed in the mild night air and thought that it was good. There was a lot to be said for night duty in weather like this, he thought. He lit another cigarette.

Devery had his own thoughts. It was getting late, too late for him to go to Ella Bowie's place, no matter how willing she was to have him call. He reflected that he had done himself a bit of good with the McQuade-Hart-Jackman business, one way and another. He would now be definitely in the running for promotion. But not if the authorities discovered that he was fooling around with the widow of Caps Bowie. They would take a dim view of that. He decided that it would be better for everybody if he did not visit Ella, that night or any other night.

Cassidy also had his own thoughts. And he had been watching Martineau. And he was a daring man when driven by what he considered to be necessity. He cleared his throat, and people waited to hear what he had to say.

''Tis a warm night, sorr,' he murmured confidentially to Martineau in his very best brogue. ''Tis a thorsty night.'

'I agree, Cassidy. I could do with a drink myself.'

'There was a case of Whitbread's ale in the kitchen.

Two dozen bottles. 'Tis a great pity. The lawyers will fool around till it has all gone bad.'

Martineau put his hand in his pocket and brought out the key of the front door. Thoughtfully he swung the key from his little finger. Champagne-and-brandy, or beer ?

'Here,' he said to Cassidy. 'Go and bring out the beer. You, Cook, go with him and bring some glasses. We don't bear anybody any malice, but the man we're going to drink to is Mick McQuade, God rest his soul.'

.   .   .   .   .

Devery was drinking his third bottle of beer when he decided that he would, after all, go to see Ella that night.

>>> If you've enjoyed this book and would like to discover more great vintage crime and thriller titles, as well as the most exciting crime and thriller authors writing today, visit: >>>

The Murder Room
Where Criminal Minds Meet

themurderroom.com

www.ingramcontent.com/pod-product-compliance
Ingram Content Group UK Ltd.
Pitfield, Milton Keynes, MK11 3LW, UK
UKHW040435280225
455666UK00003B/79